THE SEARCH FOR MARY EVELYN

A novel

Felton McLellan Johnston

Also by Felton McLellan Johnston

1952

Sycamore Crimes

In Deep

For family and loyal friends. There is no greater treasure.

CHAPTER ONE

WITHOUT A TRACE

"Sure, this is a tough assignment, Yuri, but that's why we are asking you to do it. The biggest challenges go to the ablest person, and that's you. You also know the area, and you'll have whatever support you reasonably need. You have the observation reports and the other briefings. You will have your own hand-picked team to help – a small one, but that's what you've always preferred. However, there isn't much time. The good thing is that you have two choices. Either she suffers a fatal accident – and it has to look not just plausibly but *convincingly* like an accident - or she just disappears without a trace. Without a trace, you understand. And when it's done you can go back to Svetlana and the children and have a long rest, maybe go to Sochi for a vacation, and you'll have privileges no one else in your ranks enjoys, that's certain. So good luck, Yuri, except that luck can't play a role. This has to be done right – there's no margin for failure. You understand?"

"I understand."

"So how will you proceed?"

"'Accident' – that's too complicated. - 'Without a trace'
– I can do that."

CHAPTER TWO

A TANTALIZING ITEM FOR SCOTT SINCLAIR

The year 2000 was popularly celebrated as the beginning of a new millennium even though it was really the concluding year of the old one. Still, it was a threshold year, and for Scott Sinclair, an especially eventful one, when fortune smiled on him and smirked a little too. It was the year when he sold his Capitol Hill row house, a house that he had purchased twelve years earlier as a fixer-upper, that he restored through years of mostly personal effort, and that yielded a substantial profit from a rising and gentrifying market, a profit sufficient for him to purchase a condominium apartment in a building on Embassy Row. It was a year when his professional and financial fortunes took a substantial turn for the better, a year when he made a life-changing decision, and a year when he found limits to his abilities.

His long article in *The New Yorker*, exposing and detailing the incompetence and corruption associated with a military procurement project, brought Scott attention from many quarters. He was offered speaking engagements, which he declined except for one case as a favor to a friend. Young journalists offered to work for him. He wanted and needed no help. Four major corporations asked to be subscribers to his quarterly national security newsletter, but he tailored each one to the particular client's business, and that involved much more effort than a more general publication, so he added only two to his existing four subscribers. And then there were the people who wanted to alert him to some scandal or conspiracy he ought to investigate. A man in Brooklyn wrote to advise him that aliens had taken over the minds of the Chief Justice of the Supreme Court and several key legislators, and that they were making inroads into the Executive Branch as well. Scott could almost believe it.

But most informants were people who worked somewhere in the Federal Government, seeking, usually anonymously, to interest him in some alleged wrongdoing in government. Why did they do it? People leak information to outsiders for any number of reasons: for revenge, for protection, to bring down an enemy, to make themselves feel important, and sometimes plainly to right a wrong, especially a public wrong.

Some journalists made their mark by combing through mountains of data. Scott did not, and in fact he acknowledged that he wasn't much of a researcher. His strength was to draw information from people, which led him to other people, until he had a picture of a community of actors in a story he would eventually tell about flawed and unflawed characters involved, innocently or not, in some scheme. An unexpected bonus from his recent celebrity was the surprising willingness of people who were typically somewhat guarded to share confidences or gossipy tidbits. He put that down not just to becoming well-known certain circles, but equally to the care his article showed for protecting his sources and avoiding embarrassment to the innocent, or mostly innocent.

Today, a Friday in June, when the forecast was for clear skies and a warm but not yet sweltering Washington summer day, was full of promise. Scott had his appointments lined up, and his weekend planned: breakfast at the Old Ebbitt Grill with an ambassador-nominee who wanted Scott's advice on his nomination hearing; a morning meeting at the Treasury Department with an official who could bring him up to date on some policy developments; and lunch with a former colleague on the National Security Council staff. All of these would probably yield useful information for his next newsletter.

In the Nation's Capital money always held great sway, but information was the real coin of the realm. It was hoarded and expended like any currency, used to buy influence, to gain advantage, to aid or to injure. And if you were careful, its movement, unlike financial transactions, left no trace. Information was the foundation of Scott's livelihood. He cultivated sources as an earnest farmer sows seed and tends his crops, looking to an eventual harvest. His methods varied, but in the main it was a matter of keeping up friendly relationships and building confidence in his discretion. Once having acquired a thread of promising information he gently tugged at his sources to unravel the whole fabric of secrecy and deception that cloaked the truth. He also had methods of eliciting information from recalcitrant sources, typically those who feared embarrassment or worse coming from his inquiries. Nothing heavy-handed. Usually his message was: without your version, you may look worse than you deserve.

His waking thoughts went beyond the day's business, to the evening's dinner party, to Marge Hudson's company, her conversation, and her body; to tennis with her on Saturday, to reading books and the weekend newspapers, making meals with Marge and entertaining her dog, Fay, and being entertained by her in turn. Life was good.

With the wind of success at his back and with eagerness for the day's work and play, Scott left his condominium building, a four-story Victorian mansion where he occupied the third floor, and fairly danced down the steps toward the street. His eagerness turned abruptly to wariness when he saw a figure standing on the sidewalk, a man in a worn suit that may have better fitted its original owner, and wearing a well-worn derby. The man had a large satchel slung over his shoulders, and his eyes were fixed directly on Scott's.

Panhandlers were a common sight downtown, but Scott's wasn't a neighborhood frequented by them. Maybe they were branching out, Scott thought. He braced himself for the encounter.

"Mister Sinclair, I presume," the man said cheerfully.

"How did you know?"

"Got your picture here, from the newspaper." The man's smile broadened as he showed him an article about Scott torn from a recent newspaper. "Don't worry, boss. I ain't here to put the bite on you. Got something for you."

He reached into his satchel and handed Scott a large manila envelope with Scott's name and address on it in handwritten block letters.

"What's this about?" Scott accepted it gingerly.

"Don't know, boss. Maybe a summons!" He laughed at his joke. Scott didn't.

"Well, then, who's it from?"

"Ask me no questions, boss, and I tell you no lies. I'm just a courier, and I'm not supposed to tell you who paid me to give this to you. Man gave me a Jackson just to deliver it and keep my mouth shut. Even we couriers have professional standards, you know." With that he tipped his hat, mounted a bicycle parked by a nearby tree and shouted, "You can call me Mercury!"

Scott put the envelope in his briefcase and made his way downtown on foot, relieved and amused.

"Don't worry about the hearing," Scott assured the ambassador-nominee over his eggs Benedict. "It's just pro forma. The important thing is your meeting with the chairman just before the hearing, and you may not even get that, because he's busy with other things. So, you will meet with the staff, which does count. It's a chance to develop a relationship with those people, because you never know where or when you will encounter them later on. Some of them may seem to you impossibly young, but they're not stupid, and they can be helpful. Suggest that you would welcome a CODEL at your embassy, when they could come along with their senators. Ask them some opinions. You know more about what you are about to do than any of them ever will, but let them think otherwise. You don't need to grovel – just be friendly and respectful.

It may helpful to you someday, and likewise it doesn't pay to get on their wrong side."

With that advice, and aware that he was doing with the ambassador-nominee exactly what he suggested he do with the staffers, Scott moved on to his next meeting.

In the cavernous Treasury building Scott met with a recently appointed assistant secretary in an office of a size that awed even the incumbent. Their relationship went back many years to Scott's time as a Hill staffer. Not much came of the interview because his friend was just finding his footing, but a foundation was laid for later on.

Scott conducted his last interview in Lafayette Park, on a bench over by the monument to the Marquis de Lafayette, facing the White House. He and his former colleague from the National Security Council decided that a box lunch in the park was better suited to a confidential conversation than the crowded White House mess where the utmost candor with an outside visitor was unwise. The conversation had gone well. No classified information was divulged, just some insight into the nature of some policy discussions and Administration thinking, and morsels of information of little moment by themselves but which when fitted into Scott's broader knowledge filled out a useful picture.

After lunch Scott lingered in the park. He enjoyed watching the mid-day activity – the ever-present nuclear protesters with their mobile shelters and placards confronting an oblivious White House across Pennsylvania Avenue, the comings and goings of tourists, nearly all of whom managed to take, or have taken, a photo of them with the White House in the background, and the locals, office workers, like himself enjoying the weather and an al fresco lunch. Behind him a mounted Park policeman was thrilling young children from a nearby daycare center. Scott wondered if many of these urban youngsters had ever even seen, outside of a zoo, any fauna other than the squirrels that panhandled throughout the park.

Returning his attention to his notes and recollections of the morning's meetings, Scott was gratified that he had harvested ample useful information for his newsletter, with valuable insights for his clients, and enough Washington insider anecdotes to supply a week's worth of dinner and cocktail conversations. Then he turned to that manila envelope, so mysteriously delivered. He broke it open.

Inside there was a quarter inch pile of documents covered by a plain sheet of paper with the words "THIS SHOULD INTEREST YOU" written in block letters. Obviously, the sender was taking care to be anonymous, so that even a professional investigation wouldn't reveal who he or she was. And even if he ever saw "Mercury" again, the courier would certainly stay faithful to his code of secrecy, for which Scott admired him.

Of course, this item, whatever it turned out to be, could be useless, uninteresting, or worse, deliberately false. He flipped through the pages to see if they included any classified documents. If there were, they would go straight to the FBI (after he had read them), along with any evidence of their origin, like an envelope. There were none.

The package consisted of several government memos, some accounting pages, and several printed email chains. Several documents bore cautionary but unofficial warnings like: "MOST SENSITIVE" AND "EYES ONLY." It didn't take long for Scott to get the gist of things. A multi-country foreign aid project code-named "Good Ends" was a large-budget program, closely held by a few officials, and apparently running into serious trouble. This was promising.

Scott decided there was enough time left in the day to get a running start on "Good Ends" and made his way back to his apartment where he spent an hour on his computer, gathering information that would help him develop a strategy for peeling away barriers to the truth and turning that into a major story of a government program gone awry. He drew up organizational charts, assembled backgrounds of officials whose names appeared in the documents, and built foundations for further investigation.

Then Scott walked to the post office to fire off a Freedom of Information Act ("FOIA") request to the most relevant organization, registered mail/return receipt requested. Before pursuing other avenues, he would wait a few days to see what that yielded. Back in his apartment he showered and changed clothes, filled a small carry-on bag with four bottles of wine, his laptop computer, and some clothing, and set off on foot to the Metro station where the Red Line would take him most of the way toward Marge's house.

CHAPTER THREE

SPREZZATURA

When she finally decided to end her six month's love affair with Scott Sinclair, Kirsten Devens confided in her closest friend. "Scott would make the perfect husband: decent and kind, well-mannered, cultured, wise, charming and all of that. Maybe not movie star handsome but pretty good-looking anyway. He would be a good provider. And, not to be vulgar or anything, he's very good in bed. There's only one problem. He likes being a bachelor. So, I finally decided to move on, even though the chance of meeting someone else with his qualities isn't great. Being his girlfriend was like having access to a fabulous wardrobe on loan. I'm going to miss him though."

Earlier in their relationship she, a literature professor and an authority on Renaissance poetry, had paid him this compliment: "You," she said, "have 'sprezzatura.'"

Many who knew Scott, if they happened to know the meaning of the word, would readily have agreed. Celebrated by the 16th century courtier Castiglione, "sprezzatura" referred to a quality of graceful   conduct and performance without apparent effort. But in fact, effort had everything to do with his conduct and abilities.

It was true that Scott was gifted with a quick mind and an instinct to excel and to please and had developed a multitude of abilities. He could perform the Heimlich maneuver and a few pleasant tunes on a piano. He could recite from memory the entire Bill of Rights and *Dangerous Dan McGrew*. He could write a compelling proposal or a letter of condolence with equal facility. He could fix a flat tire, a leaky faucet, or a gourmet meal when needed. He was always well and appropriately dressed. He could charm and console. And, importantly for a person so accomplished, he could suppress the instinct to shine, could stay quiet or lie low to let others take the stage.

But his apparent sprezzatura was largely a product of study, observation, practice and preparation. He learned from others. What he found admirable or attractive in other people, he studied and emulated. Did someone have a gift for story-telling or making a convincing argument? He watched them carefully, noting their techniques. He absorbed knowledge from books, articles, acquaintances, and chance encounters.

Complementing his graceful manner, Scott had mastered many practical skills, initially from necessity and Scott's inherent frugality. He had had to make do with a modest salary. A plumber once charged him a substantial sum for doing some simple task, so he taught himself the rudiments of the trade. With a little practice he found he could mend a garment that would give years more wear without an expensive trip to the tailor. He cared for his belongings to make them last. He could still wear shoes that he purchased a quarter century earlier; they looked nearly new.

Few people get through life going uninterruptedly from success to success. Failures and other kinds of loss, if they occur early in life, can be crippling or warping, or they can instill resilience, humility, empathy and prudence, qualities that come in handy for the rest of life. Scott was one of those fortunate people who absorbed the experience of failure, losing sheen off his self-confidence for a time without depriving him of it for long.

The stumbles Scott suffered he made building blocks of experience. He once failed to show sufficient deference to a senator – a particularly vain and vengeful one – and as a result was dismissed from his staff position on the Senate Foreign Relations Committee. Fortunately, this occurred as a new administration was taking office and Scott landed safely on the National Security Council staff. A book on foreign policy he authored was rejected by publishers because he lacked the academic credentials or high position that might make it sell. But only one failure was severe: an early marriage. Fueled my mutual sexual urges and blind to the disparity of their goals and values, he and Jane had rushed headlong into a short-lived marriage. Jane coveted the country club life and knew that someone as clever as Scott could give that to her. But Scott's ambitions lay toward career accomplishments that came, at that stage, with meager financial rewards. No sooner had Jane bolted to her parents' home in Tennessee than she discovered she was pregnant. Her family had the means to give their son Andrew a comfortable upbringing and Scott did not. Jane remarried a man with two car dealerships and the requisite country club membership. So Scott never became the father he meant to be and Andrew grew up, Scott feared, with their values. Scott had occasional but awkward contacts with Andrew, who was now working on Wall Street performing a kind of financial alchemy by which many risky loans could be packaged into a security that was rock solid, he said.

Scott had shortcomings too. A few women he courted dumped him because he was too old-fashioned for their taste, others because no marriage proposal seemed in the offing. He never learned to dance well. He had an ear for music but no voice. He decided early on not to learn to play bridge or chess, not having much interest in sedentary games, which took up a lot of time. Similarly, he never bothered to learn to play golf, which ate huge parts of a day, although he was a good tennis player.

CHAPTER FOUR

MARGE, FAY, AND HAROLD

Friends of Marge Hudson would describe her to you this way: energetic, can-do, problem-solver, helpful to anyone in need, fun, engaging, attractive – her looks belied her entering middle age. But, being her friends, they wouldn't share with you everything they knew or suspected, which had to do with her divorce over a year ago from Harold ("the bastard" as she privately called him), who ran off with a young paralegal ("the bimbo") in his office. Her closest friend Connie would put it this way: "Marge is the nicest person in the world, but you wouldn't want to cross her in a serious way. Harold learned that the hard way. Look, she worked her tail off and scrimped and saved to help put him through law school, and was the loyal wife for twenty-some years. Well, what would you expect a woman with spirit to do when she is betrayed, and worse in Marge's case, subjected to the public humiliation of being rejected for a much younger woman? She hired the best junkyard divorce lawyer around and stripped Harold of most of his wealth. Served the bastard right, if you ask me."

The divorce settlement enabled Marge to buy a substantial house in Potomac, Maryland, near Washington – a place with enough fenced property to accommodate a large dog. The settlement also included an investment portfolio that could have relieved Marge of any need to work, but she stayed on as headmistress of an Episcopal church-affiliated grade school, for the challenge. And she otherwise kept up a busy life. Marge hadn't needed so much out of the divorce financially – she could have lived quite comfortably on her salary and a modest inheritance from her parents – but she was only too happy to punish Harold by depriving him of a good share of their wealth. For good measure Marge jettisoned just about everything that reminded her of Harold, including his surname, "Hinckley". She never liked the name anyway. She was now Marge Hudson again.

Marge's loss, her broken marriage, which she couldn't help feeling was a kind of failure, no matter how blameless she was, came late, but her success, her ability to cope with almost everything else that was thrown at her, and the admiration others had for her, allowed her to compartmentalize that loss, so that the damage it did was so interior and not hardening, except when it came to getting even. If anything, it seemed to strengthen her in her resolve to be good at everything she undertook, and to make a life that to observers was as complete and successful as one could have, if one were a single person.

But Connie, who was close enough to Marge and discerning enough to read her thoughts, knew that she was a wounded even if otherwise strengthened warrior in the battlefield of life. It was Connie who more or less bullied Marge into getting Fay, a Great Dane, ostensibly for protection but at least as much for companionship.

Marge left her office early, school being in recess for the summer and there being no reason to hang about that day. Almost everything was in good order at the school, and what was not – a fundraising challenge, an underperforming teacher, and a student whose parents expected junior's discipline problems that began at home should be resolved in the classroom - she had plans and the skills to deal with. She knew how to cajole parents and alumni into generous giving. She knew how to coach a teacher to better performance and how to dispose of one who refused the help. And she would tell those parents that perhaps junior would be happier at a different school. That would take care of that.

One thing I'm good at, Marge thought, is compartmentalizing things. I've got my work, which certainly has its challenges, but there I'm pretty much on top of things. I've got a pretty good Board, I get along with the clergy, or at least they don't interfere much. The teachers are mostly very good, and things are stable. Other people are doing most of the heavy lifting when it comes to fund-raising. The biggest problems are the parents. Some of them think the world revolves around their particular cherub, or should. If the teachers can't appease them, they come to me. Unless you're ready to get rid of them you can't tell them that little Johnny's misbehavior or distraction might just have something to do with his home life. So be nice and be a good listener, but never give in to extraordinary demands, because that's a slippery slope.

The next big compartment was her social life, which nowadays is pretty much to say her life with Scott. Everything in that department is just about perfect. But perfection isn't permanent. Right now, she and Scott had an ideal relationship. All the parts were in order: common values and outlooks, well-suited personalities, no great disparities in social or financial matters, sexually happy with each other, no arguments or even significant differences. And no problems, except one: Scott's apparent satisfaction with things as they were. Every time the subject of marriage even appeared remotely on the horizon, nothing was said. She certainly wasn't going to bring it up. But come on, she couldn't imagine herself a permanent grass widow with a weekend boyfriend.

Maybe Scott was just afraid of commitment. Maybe things were just too easy for him this way, not having to make any compromises or adjustments to the happy life he was enjoying now. Maybe bachelorhood was the only thing he wanted. It would all be so much easier if she weren't head over heels in love with him.

After her divorce, and until she met Scott, Marge had resigned herself to a single life. It wasn't that she didn't crave male companionship - on the contrary - but she had resolved never to put herself in a position to be humiliated again. But another part of Marge wanted very much to be in a position of vulnerability. Wasn't that what romantic love was really about – trust?

When Scott appeared on the scene, showed every sign of being decent and sensitive, and had the same "let's just enjoy ourselves and not make any commitments" attitude, she decided that she could hazard a little of her dignity. Besides, Scott was cultured, easygoing, and undemanding. If he fell short of real handsomeness, having a bit too long a face and a somewhat jutting chin, he had startling blue eyes and an ample stock of sandy hair, and he kept himself in shape. He made a perfect gentleman companion. And he was reasonably well off now, so that he could not be suspected of having any particular interest in her money.

The more she knew Scott the greater her confidence in him became. And now the thought of losing him, a man who was what many a Washington woman would consider a prime catch, concerned her very much. And God knew he would never lack for companionship and society. He was a much sought-after dinner guest since his *New Yorker* article came out. Marge knew that he was turning down invitations from would-be matchmakers eager to steer him to a friend or wanting to liven up a dinner table of stale Washington society fixtures.

The threat wasn't just the possibility that some other woman would catch his eye. It was that he was so self-sufficient in every respect that she feared in the end that he might not really need her. He had been a bachelor almost as many years as he had lived before his previous marriage. Almost incidental to Marge's thinking had been sex, but no longer. She was amazed at herself, at how he had gently coaxed her into bed (hers in fact) to begin with and caused her to throw off inhibitions that she had never fully lost with her ex-husband. He had awakened in her long dormant depths of lust and brought her to the joy of abandonment to unbridled sexual indulgence with a trusted partner. Scott had offered her something much better than Harold's unimaginative and expeditious approach to conjugal relations, and it was with schadenfreude that she contemplated the bimbo's eventual realization that Harold was deficient in both wealth and bedroom skills.

Teetering on the high wire of romance, she faced the prospect of losing him troubled her more and more now. And how likely was it that, at her age (a year older than he was), she would find another man like him? However badly it had ended, she had liked being married, and when she pictured herself as an aging divorcee the image depressed her.

However attentive and constant a lover and companion Scott was, he was sending no signals about marriage. Maybe he just liked being single – he was somewhat set in his ways. Anyway, she certainly wasn't going to bring it up.

Connie would also have liked to prod Marge about her relationship with Scott, who she thought was an ideal match for Marge, but on that matter: Marge put her foot down. Their once and final conversation about that went like this:

Connie: "When are you too getting married?"

Marge: "You never beat about the bush, do you Connie?"

"Would you like to marry him? You seem to be perfect for each other. Has he asked you?"

"We haven't discussed it."

"Maybe he needs some prompting."

Marge's normal mild demeanor disappeared. "Listen, Connie, I love you and I owe you a lot, but I won't tolerate your meddling in this matter. Is that clear?"

"Sorry. Still," Connie said," I know what makes a good marriage: two people who have good characters and kindness, and enough in common. All the other stuff won't get in the way. If they don't have that, nothing else is going to make it a happy marriage. You and Scott not only have a lot in common, but you're the right kind of people. As to those issues you mentioned, you'll work them out."

"Well, first he has to propose to me. I haven't gotten even a hint so far"

"Be patient. Or maybe let him think he might lose you."

"I can't play games. Anyway, that might just make him think I don't love him." Marge fixed Connie with a firm gaze. "And don't even think of meddling, Connie. I mean it."

Entering her house in Potomac, Maryland, Marge received the usual enthusiastic greeting from Fay, a Great Dane with an imposing presence and an affectionate nature. Marge then went to the kitchen to confer with Angelina, who was readying tonight's dinner. In her bedroom Marge exchanged her pant suit for shorts, a T-shirt and running shoes, and left for a run with Fay in a nearby park.

Fay was not just a loyal and devoted companion. She was a formidable protector. In her daily walks and runs in the adjacent park land Marge feared no danger. Although Fay was docile and friendly (she had washed out of police dog training on account of her eagerness to make human friends), if she perceived a threat she shed her normally jolly manner and transformed herself into a glaring, hard-breathing black menace with a ready-to-spring posture, giving Marge confidence when she was out and about with her, or whenever anyone came unbidden to her door.

Knowing that she would respond to commands and not get into any trouble, Marge let her off leash, so that she could experience the joy of running and show anyone they passed what a splendid animal she was, all 180 pounds of her, how powerful and elegant, how disciplined, and how beautifully she ran, like a racehorse. She was glossy black, nearly three feet at the shoulder and, on her hind legs, able to look most people in the face. All friendliness and gentleness – until circumstances required otherwise.

Fay's companionship on the trail also took some of the boredom out of running, and running anyway cleared Marge's head of the issues of the working day so that she could concentrate on what was to come – the dinner party, and especially a weekend with Scott Sinclair.

Returning with Fay from the park. Marge was surprised when she saw a car parked in her driveway, and more surprised, and not pleasantly, when Harold emerged from it.

Over the months Marge's bitterness and anger had not gone away, or even much diminished, but they had been edged to a remote corner of her consciousness as her satisfaction with her new life grew. Now, with the sight of Harold, it all came surging back. She felt her entire body tighten and the blood rush upward.

"Hi Marge. I called your office. They said you left early, so I came over. Can we talk?"

"Go ahead."

"I mean inside."

"No." She turned to Fay. "Fay, sit!"

Fay was eager to meet any stranger. (Might he have a treat?)

Fay sat, watching the two of them carefully. A new situation. What to do? Wait and see.

"Look, Marge. I'll out with it then. I know I made a terrible mistake. I was awful, and I'm sorry."

Marge was unmoved. "Harold, I'm used to dealing with six-year-olds. They're transparent too. So Gail dumped you, or the other way around. Not a big surprise."

"Frankly, she turned out not to be the person I thought she was. And I also have come to realize how lucky I was to have you, and how foolish I was to leave you." Harold swallowed and said, "I want you back."

"Oh, please, Harold. That's impossible. I'm happy the way things are now. Leave me alone."

Harold lost it. "Sure, now that you've got my money." He reached out and clutched her shoulder. She drew back, but Harold didn't let go.

Fay rose from her sitting position and fixed Harold with a menacing stare. Her lips curled to reveal her impressive teeth and she uttered a low growl. Harold took his hand off Marge's shoulder.

"I hear you're shacking up with some writer now. He probably just wants your money. Excuse me, I mean *my* money."

"Harold, you'd better get moving before Fay's patience runs out. She was trained to be a police dog, and her ancestors hunted wild boars, so she knows how to handle scum balls." Marge didn't mention that Fay had washed out of that training. Anyway, she had no doubt that Fay would protect her if Harold acted more aggressively.

Fay cocked her head in anticipation of instructions. "Fay, stay." And to Harold, "I can't hold her back forever. Better get in your car and go now."

Harold got into his car, rolled down the window, and shouted, "Bitch!" before backing out of the driveway and speeding off.

Fay had resumed her sit. "He meant me, Fay, not you. Thank you."

It seemed to Marge that Harold had aged, noticeably, since she saw him last – in court where the formalities of divorce had been taken care of. Did it shame her that she took some pleasure in it? She knew that it should, but it did not.

Marge realized that Fay's presence was what kept her from being fully rattled. They went into the house and Marge presented her with the largest dog bone in the larder.

CHAPTER FIVE

SCOTT, MARGE, AND FAY

Marge liked to entertain, and many times she held impromptu Margarita parties, backyard barbecues and informal lunches. Marge never made a fuss about such gatherings of neighbors and friends. But to Marge a formal dinner party was serious business. Not that the event should be stuffy, but all aspects of the evening should be planned and carried out with a view to pleasing and genuinely entertaining all of the guests, and she expected the guests in turn to come with the same attitude. Tonight's dinner was such an occasion.

As usual, Marge had matters well in hand. Choose the menu – rack of lamb - and get out of Angelina's way in the kitchen. She had bought the flowers on the way home; she had set the table that morning before leaving the house; the bar was well stocked with her guests' preferences. Scott promised to bring a few bottles of pinot noir. But choosing the guests was the key to success. With the right mix of agreeable people, a good evening will be had by all, no matter what else goes wrong. Or almost. But with the wrong mix or difficult guests, everything else can go well but a disaster might occur. Tonight was easy.

There would be only six at the table, so there would be no difficulty with protocol or having the same genders side by side (something that she believed should not happen at the dinner table just as it shouldn't in a dogsled team), and she was reasonably confident that everyone would get along. Judge Mike McEvoy and his wife Dottie were old friends who had introduced her and Scott. It had been a happy accident nine months earlier when Scott's date cancelled on him and he invited the McEvoy's to bring a friend to fill the empty seat at the opera, where he and they had adjacent series tickets seats. Michael McEvoy, formidable and intimidating on the bench, was avuncular and agreeable off of it, and his wife Dottie would have deflated him if he were otherwise, she being a respectful spouse who saw it as her responsibility to draw the curtain of his gravity to reveal her husband's most amiable qualities.

Connie was a little risky because of her outspokenness, but Marge hoped she would be on her good behavior and even if she weren't the other guests were easygoing and likely to shrug it off. To even out the table with a male guest Marge turned to Scott, who invited Roger Harrington, an amiable young bachelor lawyer from the firm that he used mainly to keep himself on the right side of the libel laws. It would be clear that no matchmaking was intended because of the considerable age disparity between widowed sixtyish Connie and the young attorney. Finally, Marge knew she could count on Scott to anchor the opposite end of the dinner table, do bartending duty, and charm everyone.

Fay was assuming her customary place in the foyer, dozing in a head-on-paws, sphinxlike posture. She sprang up when she heard a car door closing. Marge opened the door to welcome Scott, an early arrival. Fay had grown accustomed to having Scott around the house – for months he had been spending most weekends there. Fay was allowed to rise up on her back legs and rest her front paws on Scott's upraised hands, the better to lick his face. That greeting performed, she ran to the back of the house to retrieve her frisbee and returned to present it to Scott by way of invitation to play.

"Do I get to say hello now?" Marge embraced Scott and kissed him on the part of his face that Fay hadn't reached with her tongue. "Why don't you and Fay have fun while I make myself presentable for dinner?"

Other than to shower and change into a cocktail dress Marge didn't have to do much to make herself presentable for company. She was petite and slim. Her short brown hair framed a face some described as pixyish, with a ski slope nose, eyebrows that rose high on her forehead, and a complexion that other women envied. Her personality and sense of style made her seem prettier to others than what she thought she saw in the mirror.

Marge went into the walk-in closet to choose a dress. Things there had been rearranged over the last couple of months. A corner section had been cleared of her things to make room for a suit, some slacks and a blazer belonging to Scott. There were two pair of shoes and a pair of slippers under them, and a small chest had been emptied for some of his other clothing, including his tennis outfits. Scott was spending most weekends with her.

A little makeup, the dress, a pearl necklace and earrings and Marge was ready for the evening. When she came downstairs, she found Scott in the living room with Fay again in repose after their game, with her great head resting on his foot.

"I would have come to fetch you from your stop if you'd asked." Marge restrained herself from adding sarcastically, "think of how much cab fare you would have saved." Scott's frugality was an oddity that she had grown accustomed to, and although she thought it a little extreme, she wasn't the type of person to needle people about their idiosyncrasies. And especially not Scott if it might in any way impair their relationship. Anyway, Scott was frugal but not miserly, and he was willing to spend freely on things that he cherished, like season opera tickets, certain furnishings at the right price, and quality clothing that he would make last many years. And he was open-handed with others.

Marge sat on the sofa facing him, her legs folded under her like a little girl. Fay settled opposite them, massive head on massive paws, observing their conversation, her eyes shifting back and forth to whichever person was speaking, as though she were watching a tennis match. She soon grew bored and dozed off.

"How was your day, darling?"

"Not bad. Just administrative stuff. And I met with some parents who didn't like to hear that little Bobby's constant misbehavior was unacceptable. They acted as though the problem originated in school. They thought that a different school might do a better job of dealing with him. I agreed – not what they were expecting. Problem solved. How was yours?"

"Couldn't have gone better. I got a lot of useful information for my newsletter about some coming policy and personnel changes and I'm developing a good relationship with a new source. And then I received some information about what could be a major government scandal story. Plus, I picked up some juicy gossip."

Marge shifted her position slightly and leaned into him. "Goody. I'm all ears."

"It's mostly inside baseball stuff. A senior guy at State isn't performing up to scratch in an important position, so he's being shifted elsewhere. A 'ground floor defenestration' as my informant put it. The rest is about who is sleeping with whom, who's got a drinking problem, and what bureaucratic battles are going on. The usual cut and thrust."

"Your world is more interesting than mine."

"Not really. I'm sure that human behavior is the same whether in the schoolhouse or in some large bureaucracy. But you are too decent to share the dirt that goes on at Saint Sebastian's.

"There's nothing scandalous to report. We're Episcopalians, you know!"

"Yeah, sure." They both laughed.

Marge put her hand on his. "Do me a favor, won't you? The McEvoy's are old and dear friends, and so is Connie, but they've never met before. You know Connie's the dearest person in the world, next to you of course, and she's been wonderful to me, but you know how direct she is, and on top of that she's apt to drink too much since Jack died, which is a bad combination, and I don't want there to be any, you know, friction, so please try not to let her drink too much, and since she'll be on your left at the table, kind of keep an eye – I guess I mean an ear – out if she seems to verge on offending anyone, if you know what I mean."

"I'll try. But I don't want to offend her either. I'm not going to refuse her a refill. Or throttle her if she starts to say the wrong thing."

"Well, if anyone can manage it, you will. And I've prepared the ground with Mike and Dottie. They know how good she's been to me, and how much I owe her, and she's been so lonely out there in that big house. But I don't want them to have an unpleasant evening either."

"Sure."

"By the way, thanks so much for coming up with another man for the table. Roger will be all right, won't he? I know you like him."

"I haven't seen him in action at a dinner party before, but he's clever, and genial and wise. I'm pretty sure he and the judge will get along fine. And so will you."

"Odd, isn't it, how the smaller the party the more careful you have to be?"

"Next time we'll have to set the table for twenty, just to be safe."

Marge was cheered to hear him say "we".

The guests all arrived promptly, almost tumbling over each other as they did. The McEvoy's were first, then Roger Harrington, and finally Connie, who arrived in her chauffeur-driven Bentley. Conversation was spontaneous, flowing as smoothly as the cocktails.

CHAPTER SIX

MORAL INVENTORY OVER DINNER

The conversation over cocktails covered familiar ground: vacations planned, the activities of children and grandchildren, the new opera season, laments (in two cases) about aging bodies and the prospect of elective surgeries, and of course Fay and other cherished pets. But this being a presidential election year and the identities of the likely major party nominees being pretty well assured, politics was a hard subject to avoid. The common ground around this particular dinner party group was the absence of enthusiasm for, or any extreme dislike of, either Governor Bush or Vice President Gore. It was generally agreed that Bush seemed unusually callow for a man his age, and had a little too much Texas swagger. Maybe not very bright. Gore, on the other hand, was conceded to be very intelligent, but kind of an awkward and wooden character and, as Dottie McEvoy put it, overly earnest.

As they moved to the dining room Scott was relieved that that particular conversational hurdle was safely behind them, and he figured he could relax his vigilance over Connie, who said she thought there had been much worse candidates in both parties, which was an opinion most would people would agree with.

Everyone had come with the intent to please others and tried to do so. But Connie, who was predictably unpredictable, asked a question that drew a sharp look from Marge. "Why is it that so many lawyers seem to break the law? I mean, think of Nixon and his Attorney General! I thought lawyers were supposed to be smart?"

Judge Michael McEvoy, an intimidating figure on the bench but in chambers and among friends a genial soul, took it in good humor. "I've often wondered that myself. Intelligence has nothing much to do with it. Smart people, lawyers or not, often have an inclination to think they can outsmart others. And even the smartest people have lapses in judgment." He went on to regale the company with anecdotes about cases early in his career involving supposedly clever people who ran into trouble.

Connie remarked, "I never realized there could be so much humor in a courtroom."

"Normally there isn't," the judge said, "which is why the funny moments stand out in my memory. There is a lot of grim business to be dealt with, and people's finances and their reputations, even their freedoms, are sometimes at stake.

Connie persisted. "Assuming that the system works correctly, don't people get what they deserve?"

"Even assuming that it works as intended – a big assumption – that doesn't mean people get what they deserve, whatever that is, because while what is prescribed by law or decided by judges or juries may be 'right' in the legal sense, it's rarely precisely fair in a wider sense. Even where there is discretion in sentencing, we don't really do "justice" because we can only focus on one or more particular transgressions (assuming there were any). In court, all of the good deeds in the world won't get you justice in the larger scheme of things. Conversely, the law doesn't give a hoot about awful things people do to each other if there isn't some statute that forbids it. Of course, it can't be otherwise – we're not God. But I do feel sorry for people whose otherwise decent lives are upended because of one particular lapse or error in judgment. Just think of the worst thing you have ever done. Would you like your whole life to be judged on that? If you think about it, we all have done some things that we're not proud of but we've never really been punished for, except maybe by our consciences. Or maybe I should just be speaking for myself."

A cloud of quiet and reflective gloom briefly descended over the dinner table as introspection took hold. For a few moments no one said anything as they, Scott included, took a little personal inventory of things they wished they hadn't done: a bad decision, a foolish act, something that they had done under pressure that had, through luck or circumstances, not resulted in their falling afoul of the law, or even earning public disapproval. And not all of those acts were youthful indiscretions. Scott was visited by a few such unwelcome ghosts, mostly from the pretty distant past, and none particularly grave matters except if they had caused unhappiness to someone. Still, when something brought them out from the recesses of his memory it took a while for them to retreat.

"Nice going, Mike," Dottie said, "You've made us all feel guilty and miserable about ourselves."

"Sorry. I didn't mean to. So, here's a better idea. What's the best thing you ever did, the thing that you would like to be judged on by Saint Peter at the gates of heaven? How about you, my dear?" He was addressing Dottie.

"Nothing stands out. Maybe the tutoring I do with underprivileged children. I learned a lot. Especially about my misperceptions. I used to think that most inner-city black kids were just budding criminals. I'm sure some of them are, but the kids I tutored were a little unpolished you might say but they responded so well to kindness and encouragement."

"You're not mentioning the one great thing you did, a great sacrifice for a friend, but I know you don't like me to mention it."

"That's right, I don't."

Marge was the only one other than Mike who knew.

"And you, Marge? I'm sure you can think of a lot."

Marge, who had had a moment to think, said "When I was a young teacher in middle schools, I managed to take some kids who had potential but were failing for various reasons, and I buoyed them up, gave them confidence and some challenges, and most of them turned around. I guess that's not much."

"If you were one of those kids, Marge, it was everything," said Mike. "You probably saved whole lives, or at least made them vastly better. The best teachers do a lot more than teach. Now, Scott, how about you?"

Scott was ready. "I had a great story about a prominent person's early indiscretions, which were part of a bigger story I was thinking of writing. I knew that person was a decent fellow and had done a lot of good. I abandoned the story."

"Bravo!" said Mike. "Maybe that means you won't expose the rest of us if you come across our misbehaviors."

Scott smiled. "Is there anything you'd like to tell me?"

Mike demurred. "I'll pass. You, Connie?"

"Offhand I can only think of one thing. A woman who worked for us as a cook and cleaner had an adolescent son who got into the wrong company and wound up spending two years in jail. He was basically a very nice kid. You know it's very hard to get a decent job when you come out of prison, which is one reason why so many people wind up right back there. Anyway, this woman was desperate to help her son, so I hired him as a chauffeur and general factotum, and I've been helping them get him through college part time. He's bright and he'll do well if the world gives him a second chance. He brought me here tonight."

"Brava!" said Mike again.

Eyes turned to Roger, who hesitated. "This a little hard. The best thing I think I ever did was to take a year off from law school to be with my sister when she was dying of cancer."

"That must have been very hard, and painful for you," Marge said, sensing the emotion in his voice, but resisting the temptation to take his nearby hand in hers.

"It was hard and painful, but it was also wonderful, and we had a lot of happy times then. Actually, we weren't very close growing up – in fact we were rather antagonistic toward each other. But that experience brought us together. I wish it had never happened, of course, but I will always be glad I did what I did."

Dottie McEvoy broke the awkward silence that followed. "It is now time for the judge to be judged."

"I honestly can't think of any one thing, nothing that approaches what the rest of you have done. I guess I'm not very noble."

"You don't have to have standout moments, Mike," Dottie said, "You have led a decent and honorable life, and behind that crusty behavior on the bench, when you take off those robes, you're a pussycat. You are a kind and honorable man, and everybody knows it. And a wonderful husband."

Touched but unwilling to show it, Mike deadpanned to the table, "She must have had too much to drink."

Marge called time on the emotional conversation. "Let's go in the living room for coffee and talk some more about politics. We don't have to be nice when we do that."

After the gentle evisceration of political figures other than Bush and Gore, Mike asked Scott a question. "Well, Scott, what's your next big expose going to be about?"

"I wouldn't say 'expose'. I'm not deliberately trying to dredge up scandals, just interesting stories about government and how it works, or doesn't." Scott was a bit defensive. He knew in his heart that scandal sells, and flat stories about the inner workings of government don't necessarily get you exposure in *The New Yorker*. "Something may have fallen in my lap today, or maybe not. It was delivered by an unusual courier who called himself Mercury, who refused to say who paid him to deliver it to me. It looks promising and yes, it's about what may be a scandal of some proportions. Of course, there are stories out there of things well done, honorably and selflessly done. I wish I would get more of those, even if they might be hard to sell to *The New Yorker*. And people in government, at least at the professional level, are rightly wary of being deemed 'heroes' publicly, especially if their deeds involved crossing a politician. There is a lot of good material out there that I will never see."

Connie was studying him closely. "Would it interest you to investigate something that happened many years ago, a kind of mystery that someone with your talents and knowledge could unravel?"

"Do you have something in mind?"

"I'll let you know," Connie said.

Scott had met Connie only briefly before. She was nearing sixty years old. After a few pleasantries she began to ask Scott more about his work, mainly about his methods. It fell only a little short of an interrogation. It was more than idle curiosity.

After Scott and Marge saw everyone off, they settled down together on a living room couch for an after-dinner drink. Marge was relieved that Connie had behaved herself tolerably well – she was famously outspoken and blunt. And Roger had conducted himself perfectly – appropriately deferential but not fawning toward the judge, making an impression that he was bright and amiable, which he was, in addition to being a good lawyer on whom Scott had come to rely a great deal. And his testimony about his "good deed" affirmed Scott's good opinion.

"By the way," Scott asked, "do you know what the good deed was that Dottie didn't want to discuss?"

"Not to be repeated, but here it is: Dottie gave a kidney to a friend who probably would have died without it."

"I never did anything like that, I'm afraid."

"You did a very good deed. You sacrificed your work product to protect a man's dignity. And besides, you're like Mike, you're an all-round good man."

Except, Scott thought, for the part about being a wonderful husband, a title he envied.

After dissecting the evening and satisfying themselves that all had gone well, Scott offered to help tidying up, since Angelina had gone home.

Marge leaned into him. "The hell with the dishes. They can wait until morning. Let's go to bed."

In bed Scott listened to Marge's rhythmic breathing and pondered his feelings and hers. He had always been a one-woman man, or at least one woman at a time, and he had been fond of all of them. Still, none of them occupied more than a niche in his busy life, which he realized was why sooner or later they all had moved on. But he was aware that Marge was now occupying the center of his thoughts, and that much as he enjoyed, even loved his work and his other pursuits, he was ever more eager for the hours he spent with her, and reluctant to leave her company. Marge seemed to reciprocate his feelings, but she had never hinted at marriage, and he wondered if her own divorce had soured her on the concept. After all she was a very complete person, and while she seemed to delight in his company, she had work she enjoyed, plenty of friends, and would surely be courted by others if he were absent. She seemed to relish her independence, with no regular companion other than Fay. He wondered if she felt that a husband would just complicate matters. If he proposed, would that spoil things?

CHAPTER SEVEN

LUNCH AT THE SULGRAVE CLUB

The following Monday morning Scott had a call from Connie Nelson. She said that Marge had given her his private number. Would he have lunch with her at her club someday this week? Or today? It was, she said, kind of a business matter. Scott guessed that she wanted to make sure he understood that she wasn't trying to poach him from Marge. She was too old for him anyway, but you never knew. He accepted the invitation.

The Sulgrave Club was one of Washington's oldest surviving elite organizations, a women's club on Massachusetts Avenue where much of the staff and the clientele had the looks and manners of a bygone era. Although he found it a bit fusty, Scott liked its quiet, and the dignified manner in which members and staff, many of them geriatrics, conducted themselves. Connie had chosen a corner table where they could talk privately, not that anyone would have dared eavesdrop, or even thought of it as something worth doing.

Their conversation was mostly about how she and Marge had become friends, and about her late husband, his lingering illness, and her intention to depart their mansion in semi-rural McLean, Virginia, downsize, and get a house or apartment in downtown D.C. Connie could afford to live anywhere she liked. She definitely did not like where she now lived.

"I don't know why we were stupid enough to move out to McLean. Jack wanted to build his own dream house instead of all of those houses he built for other people – although they were high-end enough. It was the worst decision we ever made. We quickly found out we had nothing in common with our neighbors, one next door being a Syrian dentist with a shrewish wife and terrible taste – their place is a gaudy eyesore – and on the other side somebody known as the mattress king. Not to be snooty but they built the biggest monstrosity in McLean, which is saying something, I tell you. On the other side of the road is another McMansion that has parties almost every night with people coming in and out at all hours. I hear a lot of Congressman go out there for fun and games, which is probably true considering some of the women I've seen coming and going. But even worse is the fact that the older residents out there hate all of us newcomers, building our outsized houses and driving up their property taxes and generally ruining their bucolic atmosphere. And we're - I mean I am – cut off from people. It's asking a lot for your friends to venture beyond the beltway to the semi-sticks for dinner, and with a widow too boot. It's a cultural desert too.

"So, I've been furiously throwing things out, giving them to Goodwill or the Salvation Army, etc., and I'll probably have an estate sale at some point. But you know, or I expect you know, how it is. You start going through old things and it's easy to get bogged down looking at memorabilia and what have you. Which brings me to my point today. I came across something from almost a lifetime ago that brought back a rush of memories and lit a kind of fire of curiosity under me. Did you ever hear of Mary Evelyn Klimov?"

Scott had not.

"At one time a lot of people had. She was my roommate, oh, thirty-odd years ago. And she just disappeared, like that," she said, snapping her fingers. "They never found out what happened to her. The police never got anywhere. There was a lot of speculation – she was involved with some high-level people in government – but after a while she was just forgotten, and the police and the press went on to other matters. Anyway, while I was madly throwing out papers and files – it's unbelievable how much useless stuff I've accumulated over the years – I came across a shoebox of letters and stuff that belonged to Mary Evelyn. Most of it is just bills and such, but there is a letter from her mother I think, and another from her sister, and a couple of love letters from some character who signed himself "H". I never showed those to the police because I didn't even know I had them, and when I eventually moved from the apartment that we shared the shoebox came with me like a stowaway in my moving boxes.

"What I'm coming to is that I feel as though I didn't do Mary Evelyn justice by overlooking that shoebox. This may sound funny to you, but maybe because other than this downsizing business and thinking about where I'm going to live next, I've had maybe too much time to ponder the matter. Which brings me to the point here: I'd like you to pick up the trail, so to speak. I can pay you well to see what you can make of this stuff and see if you can discover what happened to her."

"Connie," Scott protested, "I'm not a detective. Maybe that's what you need."

"No," Connie insisted, "it's not what I need. Look, I'm not interested in hiring some private gumshoe who'll string me along without getting anywhere. The thing is, I think whatever became of Mary Evelyn probably had a lot to do with the milieu she was in, her involvement with high government officials in the diplomatic service and that kind of thing. Now you, you understand how things work in that realm, and you would get things that no ordinary detective would. Also, I know I can trust you. In addition to the fact that I sized you up as a solid citizen, I know Marge wouldn't get involved with anyone who wasn't absolutely first class in every way."

"Thanks for the compliment, Connie, but I'm just getting started on a major investigative matter I mentioned that looks like it will take up a lot of my time. And of course, I have to keep my newsletter going. I don't know if I could take on another matter right now."

"OK, so get to it when you can," Connie said, cutting off that line of retreat.

"I'd like to help you but I'll have to think about it."

"I'll have to be satisfied with that, I guess. But to whet your interest, let me tell you a little about Mary Evelyn. How about some dessert?"

Scott declined dessert, but they had coffee, and Connie pressed on.

"I don't recall exactly how Mary Evelyn and I came to be roommates. Neither one of us had any money after college so sharing a tiny apartment made sense for us, and although we were very different, we got along just fine. I went to work for Garfinkel's in Spring Valley, which you may recall was *the* high-end department store in

Washington. Everything was high quality. And the sales staff really knew their merchandise, and their customers too, since the same people kept coming back. God, how I miss that place! Now it's a Crate and Barrel! So, while I was working my way up to being a buyer, and having no higher goals, Mary Evelyn was leading a far more glamorous life, hobnobbing with high government officials, even though she wasn't making much more money than I was."

"How did that happen? I mean how Mary Evelyn got into those circles?"

"Mary Evelyn grew up bilingual. Her mother had Russian ancestry and lived in Russia for many years. Mary Evelyn got her Bachelor's and Master's degrees in Russian language and literature too, so it wasn't hard for her to qualify as a translator. Plus, she was whip-smart, and charming, and pretty of course. It wasn't long before she was a favorite of the State Department and after working for a firm that provided them with translators, she realized her advantages and set up on her own, working as a contractor for the government, mainly for State but also for other agencies."

"What do you think happened to her?"

"Well, if I thought she was just murdered and dumped somewhere in some random crime I wouldn't be pursuing this. There were signs – signs I didn't pick up on at the time – that she was in some kind of a pickle shortly before she disappeared. Things like edginess, which was most unlike her normal self, and a lot of time spent away from the apartment, not that it was unusual for her to spend the night with a man somewhere, but she went out of town several times, for days at a time, and not always on one of her translator gigs overseas. But other than that, I hadn't a clue. Then I came on this shoebox of letters and things, which I want to give you. I'm hoping you can make something of it."

"As I said, I can't get to it right now."

"Understood. I can wait. I've waited all these years. Now, I know you don't use a car. I can give you a lift to your place if that's where you're headed now."

"Thanks, I accept your offer."

The walked out of the club and found Connie's car waiting for them. The chauffer opened the rear door and Connie climbed in, saying "Jeffrey, this is Mr. Sinclair. We're going to drop him off at his apartment." Jeffrey, a short, cheerful looking fellow in his 20's wore a gray suit. He gave Scott a warm smile and touched his cap. Inside

Connie passed him a shoebox with "HAHN'S SHOE STORE" printed on the cover.

"Oh, and I put in a couple of articles that were written about her when she disappeared. Call me whenever you're ready to begin and I'll send you a retainer. Name your terms and we can have a contract if you like. Of course, I will cover any expenses you may have, and don't hesitate to go first class." Scott had bought some time, but saw he was trapped.

At the entrance to his apartment house Scott thanked Connie for lunch and the lift. Jeffrey opened the car door for him. Some people in a neighboring apartment were coming out of the entrance and took note of the scene: Scott emerging from the chauffeured Bentley and an older woman smiling and waving goodbye to him. People will draw their conclusions, thought Scott. But he had a different concern: that although he had tried to dodge this assignment, he had somehow been hooked.

CHAPTER EIGHT

CONNIE REFLECTS

Connie sat in her kitchen on a barstool, leaning on the "informal dining island" that the decorator had convinced her and Jack would be a nice touch for treating informal guests to a snack and a drink. What a dumb idea, and it would have been even if she weren't stuck out here by herself. It was amazing that she, and Jack especially, who designed and built houses himself, for God's sake, had used such poor judgment when they built this monstrosity. Never build a dream house, she thought; it's just as likely to turn out to be a nightmare.

She fingered the thank-you card that her granddaughter had sent, after two months, thanking her for her birthday presents. In block letters that screamed how painfully they had been formed and wandered irregularly across the page, it said: "Thank you for the dol and the book. I like them very much, expecially the dol, which is very pretty. Love, Annie." Connie could imagine Annie's laboring away on her note under her mother's instruction. Did her mother notice the misspelling, or did she just decide that it had been struggle enough to get the child to write the note, and maybe Grannie would find it charming that way? Well, she and the child had never really bonded anyway, what with the child away in Singapore with her parents these last three years.

Connie had two daughters. She got along with them well enough, but on the other hand they weren't exactly close, which she thought was mostly her fault. She and Jack had been good parents in the sense that they were kind to their girls and saw to their wellbeing, but they had never been the kind of parents who put their children foremost in all things, which was the kind that all of them seemed to be these days. She and Jack raised their girls the way they had been raised, according to a few simple rules: see that they get a decent education, as far as they are able; try to do no harm; don't fight in front of them; let them have their way as long as they aren't exposed to too much danger. But she and Jack had been too much involved with each other, it turned out, and not enough with them, to expect them to be doting children. I put all my eggs in Jack's basket, she thought. And now look, Jack's gone, and I really have nobody, not even physically close, with the other daughter in Texas with her husband. But what's done is done.

Her only close friend was Marge. Connie was honest with herself: I'm not everyone's cup of tea. I'm opinionated and outspoken. And blunt, to a fault. Well, I'm not likely to make myself over at this point. Still, I'm not helping myself to have a social life as long as I'm stuck out here.

She would like to be married again. Or at least to have a man. She hadn't lost interest in sex. But it would have to be a man who could put up with her. Jack did, but he also kept her in check. He wasn't a man to be ruled, and when push came to shove, she yielded to his correction, maybe after a little fight, because he was usually right about things, and fair. How to find a man with that right balance? Hell, how to find any man at her age? Sixty! It sounded so much worse than fifty-nine for some reason. She considered her assets. At least she wouldn't be a financial burden to a man, but her very wealth was a kind of barrier; she didn't want any man who might be interested in her for her money. And the pool of eligible men dwindled almost daily. She seemed to be surrounded by widows, including grass widows. She envied Marge, who had everything – financial independence, looks, an interesting and responsible job, a great personality and lots of zip. And a man, even if not a husband. Well, as for herself she had the independence, and she thought she was holding up pretty well and wasn't bad looking - for sixty.

As for Marge, her dear, loyal and admired friend, Connie couldn't understand how she hadn't snapped up, or been snapped up by Scott. My God, Scott had everything. Except Marge. And vice-versa. And here they were, cohabiting on weekends, obviously in love and ideally suited. Maybe she shouldn't have gotten Marge that dog. Maybe Fay was enough of a companion to get her from weekend to weekend. On the other hand, maybe Scott was the problem, because Marge couldn't – and certainly wouldn't – take the initiative. Still, a smart woman like Marge should be able to maneuver him into asking the question, or at least figuring out that he never would, and then move on. If she still wanted to.

CHAPTER NINE

A VISIT FROM THE FEDS AND A DEAD FOX
OFFER

In his apartment office Scott set the shoebox on a shelf and turned to the matter of more immediate interest. He was sifting through the Good Ends documents thinking about whom he would contact next when his phone rang. Scott relied on "caller ID" to spare himself the usual sales calls, which he ignored. This one commanded his attention: "Federal Bureau of Inv." The small screen on the phone accommodated only so much text, but this was sufficient. He picked up the receiver.

"Mr. Sinclair?"

"Yes."

"FBI. I'm agent Harriman. We'd like to have a chat with you about a matter we know you are interested in: 'Good Ends.'"

"I'm free right now. Can you come to my apartment?"

"Agent Blair Brown will be there within half an hour."

"I'll buzz him right up."

"Not him. Her."

Blair Brown was there in fifteen minutes. She wasn't exactly what Scott expected, but then Scott had only a Hollywood image of an FBI agent, and none at all of female agents. Agent Brown was thirtyish and might have turned heads if she had not deliberately made herself as plain and professional looking as possible: the slightest makeup, blond hair pulled back and bobbed at the back, a gray pantsuit with the jacket covering a plain white blouse, and no more adornment than a slender gold chain around her neck, and a wedding band and an engagement ring with a miniscule diamond. She flashed her badge and handed him her card.

Scott brought her into his living room and offered her a place on a sofa while he took a facing chair.

She got right down to business. "I understand that you submitted a FOIA request for information about a project called Good Ends."

"I did."

"We'd like you to withdraw it, or at least ignore the matter for now. To come to the point, we're in the middle of a significant investigation about the project, and we're afraid outside inquiries at this point might disrupt our efforts. I know a FOIA request can be declined when there is an investigation underway, but it would be more convenient for us if you just withdrew it and let the matter go for a while."

"Ms. Brown, I don't want to disrupt anything, but an investigation like this, mine I mean, is how I make a living. If I withdrew every time the authorities wanted to call me off, I might as well take up a different line of work."

Blair didn't seem surprised. "Understood. So, we have a proposal. You stand back until we are close to winding this up and then we'll give you priority access to what we have developed, before anyone else on the outside, and we'll give you plenty of detail unless it would jeopardize legal proceedings. In effect, we'll do a lot of work for you, and you get the story."

This bargain didn't much appeal to Scott, however reasonable it sounded.

"That's a dead fox."

"Huh?"

"Have you ever seen one of those movies that show a group of English aristocrats on horseback, wearing red coats, in front of the manor house, with a bunch of excited hunting dogs milling around and baying as they are about to set off on a fox hunt? Now imagine the gamekeeper showing up with a dead fox, saying, 'No need to trouble yourselves, my lords. Here's a nice dead fox for you, and everyone can go home.'

"So you're offering me a dead fox after I've been denied an opportunity to be in the hunt. I'd get a sterile narrative in proper legal/bureaucratic jargon. And I'd be deprived not only of the pleasures of the hunt, but of the warp and woof of the story, the human factors and the back- stories that give life to a mere rendition of facts."

"I get the point, and very colorfully put," Blair said. "But there would be one big compensation. You will have established a positive and valuable relationship with the FBI." She paused to let that sink in.

Scott got two messages from it. First, "You really don't want to have a negative relationship with us, do you?" The second was more promising, and Blair reinforced it. "I'm not saying that we're going to turn over the keys to the Bureau. We have rules to follow, as you know. But I expect that someone in your business is going to have times when a helping hand at the FBI could be most welcome."

For a moment Scott said nothing. Blair pressed on. "And I think I can arrange for that message to be reinforced with a high-level call, if you want that."

Even though there was a risk that Blair was promising more than she could or would deliver, this was potentially a valuable contact, one that Scott might nurture into a relationship.

"That won't be necessary. I take you at your word."

"That's great." Blair stood up. "This certainly isn't like my usual official call. Don't fail to call me in I can be of any help, you know, within bounds. If you keep your end of the bargain about Good Ends, we'll keep ours."

"Fair enough, Agent Brown."

"Call me Blair."

Scott shook her hand. "Scott."

Blair had been scanning the room all along. "This is a gorgeous place. So many beautiful things." She did not say "Must have cost a fortune," but Scott knew it must be in her mind.

It was a strikingly attractive room, with fine if eclectic furnishings. The sofa she sat on was Victorian, Scott occupied one of two Louis XVI chairs, and they were separated by an art deco coffee table, all atop a Persian carpet. When Scott could come by an item he liked he cared little about harmonizing styles so long as there could be enough color harmony, or not great disharmony. Upholstering in red, white and yellow floral patterns with substantially matching curtain and carpeting colors overcame stylistic clashes.

"There's scarcely any piece of furniture or decoration that I didn't get second hand."

"You're kidding!"

Scott wasn't typically boastful but he did take pride in the manner in which he had acquired what everyone regarded as a remarkable if eclectically furnished apartment. "It took years and a lot patience scouring estate sales, auctions and even Goodwill outlets to get most of these things. Of course, a lot of them were not in great shape when I got them, but with some help from various artisans and a bit of my own elbow grease I brought them back to life. I got that mahogany dining room table for almost nothing when all it really needed was a new set of legs and some work to bring up the finish. And I notice you were looking at the painting over the mantle."

"I sure was. It's really remarkable."

The painting, which was nearly the full width of the mantelpiece, was a view of the east face of the Capitol Building at sunset. In the foreground there were some tree limbs and lamp posts, and behind the building the sky was lit a pinkish blue.

"I'll tell you a story about it. That painting originally cost someone about $25,000, but when I found it, it was selling for only $500 because the canvas had been badly torn down there around the bottom left edge. I bought it, found an expert in restoration at the National Gallery who moonlighted repairing damaged paintings, and paid him $1,000 to fix it. I don't think anyone but an expert could see that it had been badly damaged once."

Blair was impressed. "My husband and I could stand to take lessons from you. We just bought a little house in Glover Park and we have the barest of furnishings – and unfortunately we like nice things, a lot, and with him being a teacher and me on a government salary we can't afford to pay for the things we want, at least not for a long time. Meanwhile we make do with our parents' hand-me-downs and a few odd pieces - really odd in some cases - but we'll make do with that and wait until we can afford things, we really want rather than compromise the standards we aspire to. Blair caught herself. "I'm afraid I sound kind of pompous. It's just that your example inspires me."

Scott decided that he liked Blair and that he might as well further nurture their relationship in hopes of future benefits, perhaps cementing the vague assurances of FBI friendship. And he thought of Connie and her need to downsize. "Tell me about some of the things you would most like to get now. Perhaps I can be of some help."

"That's a kind offer, Scott. Just about everything, or anything. If you could just give us some tips that would be a great help."

"I'll get back to you on that. That's a promise."

Scott saw her out the door. Although he had been deprived of a promising opportunity, he satisfied himself that he didn't come up emptyhanded. Every new friendship had a value, and who knew what some day might come of this one? Also, he liked Blair, and it was in his nature to be helpful.

It was true that Scott's acquisitions were the product of zealous bargain-hunting. He had regularly browsed estate sales and consignment stores, and even attended some auctions. He was patient. He might wait years for the right thing to show up at the right price. But he couldn't have afforded to buy and refurbish most of these items if he hadn't practiced some rigorous economies in other aspects of his life.

Not cheap, Scott simply practiced a prudent frugality. A pair of shoes could last a lifetime. But they needed to be good shoes, which were expensive, and they had to be well cared for. In the end the initial cost was justified. One of Scott's most cherished possessions was a pair of wing-tipped shoes he had purchased when he was in college.

Another economy was transport. Scott owned no car. He knew the local transit system in detail – its routes, schedules, and likelihood of delays. Therefore, no automobile purchase cost, operating cost, insurance, etc. Taxis when needed, mostly for courting. No sports club membership: Scott kept a set of weights in his bedroom and went for a run in Rock Creek Park's extensive trails and paths several mornings every week. He was fit. He subscribed to the *Washington Post* and the *New York Times*, and he found ways to get access to the Wall Street Journal when there was something there of particular interest. He was a regular at the public library, mainly for magazines (including his customer, *The New Yorker*). And he knew Washington's vast free educational and cultural opportunities, especially the Smithsonian Institution's many museums. But if the object was worth it, Scott spent. His season tickets to the Washington Opera for two were no small expense.

When he was working as a staffer on the Senate Foreign Relations Committee he used a modest inheritance from his father to buy what many would regard as a tear-down house on Capitol Hill but that he saw as a fixer-upper, although the fixing-up took more energy and time than he expected. Now, with his fortunes greatly improved by his recent article and book about the procurement scandal and by the sale of his Capitol Hill house (in its now gentrified neighborhood), he had moved to his upscale condominium apartment on Massachusetts Avenue's Embassy Row, bringing with him the artwork and furnishings he had accumulated over years of careful economy and opportunistic splurging.

CHAPTER TEN

CONNIE'S COMMISSION RECONSIDERED

Scott saw Blair out and returned to his home office, a small room that doubled as a library. He had enough to do, readying his quarterly national security newsletters whose six corporate subscribers were what kept him comfortably afloat. He had the newsletter pretty much down to a routine, enabling him to take on big investigative projects like the procurement scandal as well. But he had just lost, for now at least, his only current blockbuster prospect. He had also lost an excuse not to pursue Connie's project. It sounded as though he would be well rewarded for his efforts on that one, and Marge would be pleased if he could accommodate Connie's wishes. He would take a stab at it, and if he came to an early dead end, he would do it *gratis*.

Scott took the shoebox off the shelf and reviewed its contents. As Connie had said, there were some bills and junk mail. It appeared that Mary Evelyn was responsible for the apartment telephone bill, and then there was a department store bill, a fashion magazine, and a *Washington Post* subscription renewal invoice. Scott also found some newspaper clippings and a portrait photo of what also must have been Mary Evelyn. He could see why she was appealing to men. Scott set those aside. There was a handwritten letter that appeared to be in Russian, in the Cyrillic alphabet. Maybe he would get it translated later. There was also a letter from Mary Evelyn's sister. Two love letters were from one person, handwritten, on expensive stock with matching envelopes, no postmarks and no return addresses, and undated. The first one was short. At least he could read this one.

Dearest Evie:

You know how difficult it is for me to be unable to be with you more than I can. I just need time to unravel my circumstances so that that can change. Meanwhile we must be very careful, and I don't mean just being discreet about our relationship. There is danger for us both. Be strong. We'll work through this eventually.

All my love,

H

The other letter was somewhat longer.

Dearest Evie:

I'm so sorry that we found ourselves in that awkward situation last night. I suppose we should be grateful that it turned out as well as it (apparently) did. I don't think anyone suspects. As to the other matter, I think things are going as planned and you are doing an important service to your country, a service, I am sorry to say, that can never be publicly known.

I do have concerns about the matter of your father. Although I wish you hadn't brought your mother into this, I think she is right that you are probably being hoodwinked. It's best not to get engaged with these people any further anyway. Let's stick to our official/unofficial agenda.

It looks as though our next mission will come up soon. Something for both of us to look forward to.

All my love,

H

Scott wondered which letter was written first. They were both undated. Next Scott took up a letter that was from Mary Evelyn's sister. The envelope bore a postmark: May 3, 1970.

Dear Evie:

Thank you so much for visiting me at the convent with Mom. It was so wonderful to see you, and you looking so beautiful!

Our mother taught us at all times to be realistic and I am not afraid to face facts, or "to call a spade a spade" as you like to put it. So I face the future, dark as it seems to be, with clear eyes. In my case, though, I face it without fear, because of my faith. What is hard for me to deal with though is my concern for you. Even though we have taken very different paths (and I am not faulting you for yours, as I hope you will not fault me for mine), I feel that we are so much a part of each other and, however contrary to my faith it may be, I want to continue somehow to live through you. Also, the time may come when you may need to care for Mom – unlikely as that may seem given how strong a person she is, and how she has always protected us and looked after us – so you must look after yourself so that you can do that if the need arises.

So do take care of yourself – your wonderful, beautiful self – for my sake, for Mom's, and your own.

I will love you always,

Ellie

Scott looked at the newspaper article with a captioned photo from the society pages of the *Washington Post*. The photo was taken at some diplomatic party and it included a picture of several men in formal wear and two women in gowns. One of the women was clearly Mary Evelyn;

her image matched the photo. The caption identified three of the other people, a foreign ambassador and his wife, and someone named Ambassador Harlan Van Horn. The other article, dated July 16, 1970, was about Mary Evelyn's disappearance. It was brief, with just a thumbnail sketch of her life. It referred to her work as a translator and mentioned her attractiveness and popularity among senior State Department officials, but there was no speculation as to what happened to her nor any useful factual information. A police spokesman was quoted as saying, "We will continue to investigate, but we currently have no leads. Maybe she'll turn up one of these days." The police clearly were giving up, thought Scott. The article mentioned that a friend described her as "unpredictable and having a very adventuresome spirit." The article carried the byline of Stanley Greene.

CHAPTER ELEVEN

A GRISLY POSSIBILITY

Scott contacted a friend at the *Post* and who told him that Stanley Greene had retired to Florida. Scott called him there.

Scott had been finding that his *New Yorker* article was gaining him recognition in many quarters. Once he convinced Greene that he was not a salesman or a charity fundraiser, he repeated his name.

"*The* Scott Sinclair? I'm honored! What does a world-class investigative journalist want with a retired hack like me?"

"You're no hack, and they still think the world of you at the *Post*," Scott soothed. Then he acquainted him with his mission. "Is there anything you could tell me about Mary Evelyn's disappearance that didn't make it into your reporting?"

"Not much. There were rumors about her love life, or love lives. She was said to sleep around a bit, including with some State Department officials, but you often hear that kind of gossip or speculation when someone disappears. Me, I think she fell victim to some murderous crazy in

DC, a random victim. She had a reputation for being kind of reckless. And in particular she used to run in Rock Creek Park, especially at dusk, which is exactly what no woman should do, and she wouldn't stick to the paved trails either. That park occupies two thousand forested acres in DC and had miles of paved trail and God knows how many informal ones. I know because I wrote an article about it once. There are plenty of places for a dead body to lie undiscovered for years, except by scavenging animals." Stanley Greene had the reporter's eye for striking images.

Scott thanked him and gave him his number in case he thought of anything else later. A few days later he received from Greene a copy of an article he had written. Scott read it. It made him uncomfortable.

A Madman in the Park

Rock Creek Park runs north/south through the center of Washington, like a jagged dagger pointed at the Potomac River, splitting the city in two. It provides recreational opportunities to strollers, joggers, bicyclers, picnickers and in one location even horseback riders. There are Creekside trails and other, informal paths within the park area. It has places for quiet contemplation and for raucous celebration. And for murder.

Not that murder and other crimes are frequent. For a metropolitan park, Rock Creek has a fairly low crime rate. But low crime isn't no crime, and over the course of five years, there are likely to be one or two violent deaths, plus a few unfatal assaults. In the last four years there have been at least three deaths, *and possibly more we don't know about.*

Darryl Bantham was arrested in May of 1973 on suspicion of murdering Isabelle Symth, who had disappeared weeks earlier. Her partially decomposed body was discovered in a shallow grave in Rock Creek Park not far from where a portion of it – her left hand up to the wrist – was brought pridefully by a dog, which had briefly ventured off trail, to its horrified owner. That led the authorities to question people who frequented that portion of the park about anyone they had encountered there in months. Several of those interviewed reported that they had often come across a man who looked like some sort of naturalist, and whom they had not seen there for weeks. He was always friendly and seemed to be gathering plant specimens. But some saw him elsewhere in the park since, carrying the same worn backpack others had described. A park policeman, armed with his description, came across him early one morning, digging something up on hillside a few feet from the trail, which was a minor infraction of park regulations.

Bantham was polite and did not resist the policeman's request to inspect his backpack, a rather large one as those things go. In addition to the collapsible shovel he had been using there was a notebook, several specimen jars, a mason jar that contained a damp cloth that smelled like chloroform, a well-sharpened long knife in a sheath, and a wire noose fitted out with wooden handles. The officer took Bantham in for questioning. Faced with the inevitability of his arrest, Bantham soon confessed that he had indeed done away with Miss Smyth early on a Sunday morning as she took her customary run in the park. He said that he was not acquainted personally with her, but that they had spoken several times when he encountered her on her run, which was how he apparently built her confidence in him to a degree that she abandoned all caution when he offered to show her some interesting trailside flora.

It was as if a boil of hidden pride had been lanced, because Bantham, whose fate could hardly be compounded now, confessed to doing away with three other Washington women who, over the course of three years, had gone missing. He was able to recall where he had disposed of two of those three, but as to one victim he had no clear recollection, she being his first victim, back around 1970.

Scott scanned the rest of the article, which described Bantham's life and personality: his upbringing in a family distant from society and his parents evidently lacking in normal affection for their children; his frustration at being unable to afford to pursue his botanical interests toward a college degree; his social isolation; his employment in a statistical section of a government agency, where he made no real friends but was considered a diligent and well-mannered worker. A few noticed that while he was a rather short man he was very muscular, especially his forearms.

Scott was disappointed to learn from Greene's article that Bantham died in prison in 1988, so that he would be unable to interview him, if that would even have been possible.

Bantham's ghastly acts weighed on him. He didn't tell Marge about the article, and he decided not to tell Connie either. But the next time he spoke to Marge, he had a question.

"Do you always have Fay with you when you go for a run?"

"Almost always. Once when she was at the vet for several hours, I didn't, and I guess there may have been other occasions. Why?"

"I want you to make me a promise. Don't ever go in the park without Fay. It could be dangerous."

"I'm a big girl, Scott. What set this off?"

"Please, do me just this one favor."

"OK. I promise. Cross my heart and hope to die."

He would have preferred just "I promise."

Marge was not troubled by his intrusiveness; rather, she was pleased and encouraged by his display of concern for her.

CHAPTER TWELVE

MORE WORRISOME FACTS ABOUT MARY EVELYN

Scott made a couple of calls in search of someone who could translate the letter in Russian. He got a name, Robert Potter, a retired CIA analyst and translator, who was described to him as "an interesting character, fluent in Russian, discreet, and he knows a lot." Scott called him, described what he needed, and proposed a meeting. Potter suggested lunch at a Chinese restaurant downtown. No problem for Scott, a devotee of Chinese cuisine, and not merely because it was inexpensive.

Scott asked "How will I recognize you?"

"I bear a remarkable resemblance to that actor, Cary Grant," Potter said, "but in order to avoid the paparazzi, I typically go in disguise as a portly sixtyish gentleman with a beard and spectacles. Anyway, I'll make a reservation, so they will steer us together."

The restaurant "Szechuan Won's" was already crowded by the time Scott arrived. Potter's name drew instant recognition from the staff and Scott was directed to a table for two where sat a goateed gentleman of ample girth and a jolly countenance: Santa Claus in mufti.

"Mr. Sinclair, I presume."

"The very same. Your disguise suits you well."

Potter grinned. "Let's order. Won likes to turn the tables over here at lunch time. If we have more to talk about after lunch we can go for a walk, which my cardiologist encourages anyway." They came quickly to agreement on what to order and to share – crispy fried shredded beef for Scott and shredded pork in garlic sauce for Potter.

Scott leaned forward and began speaking in a low voice to discuss the business at hand.

"I find," Potter interrupted politely while pouring them both tea, "that if you want to have a confidential conversation at a restaurant, you can whisper, but that just invites attention and it's hard for me to follow in a busy place like this where the conversational din is so great. No one can make out what you are saying if you speak in a normal voice anyway. Not that anyone is likely to care."

Scott spoke up. "OK. As we discussed, I need a translation of a letter, and based on what I'm told about you, you may have some insights about the background – about Mary Evelyn Klimov, as I said, and those times."

"I met her once or twice, and you don't readily forget a woman like that. A real looker, and very charming too. I saw her at some meetings where she was doing simultaneous translations. And of course, I was around at the time she disappeared, not that I have any insights about that at this point. 'Foul play'? I have no idea. But I can tell you this much: she was in the middle of a lot of quiet diplomacy with the Russians, working with a guy at State named Harlan Van Horn. You might have heard of him if you were around then, but he's kind of dropped out of sight."

A fast eater even while carrying on a conversation, Potter by now had made short work of most of his pork and a good share of Scott's beef. Potter declined dessert. "I never eat dessert in a Chinese restaurant. Besides, I'm not allowed." They read their fortune cookies.

Potter read his first. "Mine says: 'You may have a challenge ahead of you'. Who writes this crap, I wonder? I'm waiting to open one that says: 'You will have a beautiful naked woman in your bed tonight' or 'Someone is planning to kill you.'"

"I hope it's the former and not the latter."

"If it's the former it will be the latter. My wife would kill me."

"Anyway, maybe this letter will keep you occupied tonight while you wait for that woman. I don't know if it will suggest anything but at least I will know what it says."

Potter read the letter quickly. "Wow. She certainly was in some kind of a pickle, or maybe more than one pickle, according to the letter. It's to Mary Evelyn from her mother. This is fascinating stuff."

"How long do you think it will take you to translate it?"

"About ten minutes if you don't mind a rough handwritten translation. We can walk over to Farragut Park and I can do it on the spot. It's a grand day to be outdoors and Won needs this table."

That they did, seated on a bench facing Admiral Farragut. While Potter penciled his translation, Scott watched the midday crowds eating their lunches and the pigeons scouting for crumbs. Several were competing for a roost on the Admiral's head and shoulders, which were dappled with pigeon waste. "*Sic transit Gloria mundi,*" Scott thought.

"Here you go." Potter tore a page from his loose-leaf notebook and handed it to him. "You'll probably want to reflect on this a bit. It certainly ought to give you a lot to chew on. It sounds like Mary Evelyn Klimov was in a heap of trouble, or at least her mother thought so. If you don't mind me holding on to this copy of the letter, I may come up with some more thoughts about it."

"By all means." Scott had no reservations. Potter had been recommended as a close-mouthed fellow, as should be the case given his profession. "And thanks. How much do I owe you? My client, that is."

"You paid for lunch. That's enough. It's nice to feel useful in your field when you're retired, not that I'm fully retired, because my wife and I have a couple of small businesses we run. Anyway, I'm as intrigued with this as you are, so, within the bounds of your engagement with your client, I'll be glad to learn what you discover."

"I'd like to do that, but as you say it will be up to the client." Unsaid: "And my conscience."

Nevertheless, Scott wanted to give something to Potter by way of appreciation, and to keep him engaged.

When he returned to his apartment Scott took out Potter's translation of the letter and read it, and then read it again.

Dearest Evelyn:

The roundabout manner in which this will reach you ought to convince you of just how seriously I take the dangers that confront you. You do not understand what these people are capable of. You have too many enemies, and you are involved in situations that could have very bad results for you. And there is the urgency of the situation. Every day, every moment increases the danger, so I beg you to do as I suggested. I know something about surviving threats and hazards, and sitting around hoping things will turn out is no solution.

If you will not think of yourself, think of me. I brought you and your sister into this crazy world amid uncertainty and danger, risking much to give my daughters freedom and security (or as much security as one can hope for in life) and now I am losing dear Eleanor and facing the possibility of losing you. I can bear a lot, and I have, but I could not bear that. Make haste!

Your anxious and loving mother.

Scott had a lot of questions. Who were "these people" and why did they pose an imminent threat to Mary Evelyn? What was the "roundabout manner" in which her mother wrote to her? What course had her mother suggested? It certainly looked like Mary Evelyn had more to worry about than the crazed denizen of Rock Creek Park. He made a copy of Potter's translation of the letter and mailed it to Connie. Then he called Connie, told her about the letter, and asked if she would authorize him to give Potter a check for $1,000, and explained why he thought it a worthwhile investment as well as compensation for work performed. She readily agreed.

CHAPTER THIRTEEN

A VISIT TO FIREWATER FARM

Scott's call to Harlan Van Horn was intercepted by Harlan's wife, Cathy. At first rather cool, she changed her tone when she recognized his name (she was an avid *New Yorker* reader), but she remained wary. Scott said he intended to write about U.S. diplomatic efforts to reduce tensions with the Russians in the pre-Gorbachev era, and about the people who played prominent roles in those efforts, like Harlan. What he told her had started as a guise and had become the truth. Scott thought it would make an interesting story, and that eased his conscience. Cathy said she would get back to him. After checking with friends who would know about such things and determining that Scott could be taken at his word and was discreet, she called back and invited him to visit them at their horse farm in Howard County, Maryland, an hour or so from Washington, and to stay for lunch. In fact, Cathy became eager to see Scott, in part because she saw an opportunity, if a somewhat risky one, to get her husband the accolades she thought he deserved, however belatedly. She also contemplated how pleasant it would be to tell her friends, whom she visited regularly in New York and Philadelphia ("for R and R" as she put it), about her connection to the now well-known writer. Scott's name had gained cachet in places he had never expected.

Close to Washington as their place was, it was a rural world away. Scott, in a rental car, admired the scenery - gently rolling hills, with working farms showing early signs of an eventual harvest - but as he neared his destination the landscape yielded to pastures, sturdy white fences that marked boundaries and restrained animals, and proclaimed rural gentrification. This was horse country.

Like many of their neighbors', the Harlan's' property served two of their passions: horses and the avoidance of taxation. Breeding and boarding horses brought in just enough income to satisfy the IRS's flexible standards qualifying their hobby as a business. An arch atop stone pillars marked the open gateway to "Firewater Farm" as a sign on one pillar proclaimed. A long drive between two white fences led to a circular drive and a sprawling single-story house that was small only in proportion to the surrounding property. At the sound of his tires crunching the stone drive Cathy Van Horn emerged from the house to greet him.

Cathy Van Horn, about 50, Scott guessed, wore a colorful print skirt and a crisp white blouse. He would not have called her pretty, but she was striking: tall, with ash blond hair and a complexion that was unmarred by the sun. A too prominent nose and a mouth a little bit too wide robbed her of beauty, but gave her a distinctive and memorable look. She had kept her figure, and her carriage signaled self-assurance. She exuded vitality.

"Welcome. I'm Cathy. I hope you didn't have trouble following my directions."

Scott took her out-stretched hand. "Scott. No problem and I enjoy getting out into the country."

"Sorry to have been so hesitant when you called, but I have to shield Harlan from some things. I should alert you that he's not in great shape. And you may find him a bit frosty at first. He's wary of journalists. We'll have our cocktails and by lunchtime he'll warm to you. That's just the way he is. Then you'll need to make the best of your time with him because he fades in the afternoon and retires for a nap. He's not in the best of health. After that we can chat together if you like. Please come in."

The house was an unusual building of stone and wood painted white, with floor-to-ceiling glass windows and doors nearly the full width of the back of the house, which sat atop a hill that looked out over the shallow-valleyed pasture below and beyond to some rolling hills. The view was only slightly marred by a power cut through one distant hillside. Cathy steered him to the living room and a brightly patterned sofa, while she took a side chair.

"As I said, Harlan's a bit wary of journalists – of course you're not just a journalist – but anyway, if you approach him in the right way, he'll be all right. I'm counting on you not to write anything critical about him."

"On the contrary, I'm thinking of him as a man ahead of his time, and an able diplomat."

Cathy smiled at the reassurance. "And speak of the devil."

Harlan Van Horn entered the room as if ready to do battle. He proved to be just as gruff and wary as Cathy had predicted. He offered a halting hand, said "Good morning," and settled into a wing chair. Cathy was right. He was not in the best of health. Although seventy-something, a good twenty years Cathy's senior, Harlan looked eighty or more if he looked a day. He had the aura of a man somewhat soured on life, bewildered at the cruelties of time, and resentful of his dependence even while grateful for his wife's support. Scott wondered if a vigorous and eventful life made old age especially hard to bear. Harlan had been gotten up by Cathy to the degree that he would tolerate: slacks, an open neck buttoned-down shirt and tweed coat, and slipper-like shoes. He was imperfectly shaved, with little whisker outcroppings here and there, and somewhat ragged fingernails, all indicating that Harlan either had difficulty looking after himself or just didn't particularly give a damn.

"I have a number of friends at State who remember you well and hold you in very high regard, Mr. Van Horn."

"Who are they?" Van Horn was not to be so easily tamed.

Scott drew out a couple of names who had told him they vaguely remembered Van Horn.

"I don't recall either of them."

"They were younger then and you might not have noticed them, but they knew you, and they knew you were doing important work. That work is what I'm here to learn more about."

"You see, Harlan!" Cathy said brightly.

Scott was glad Cathy was there to smooth the way. "I'll get the cocktails while you boys talk. I'm having gin and tonic and Harlan always has scotch and water, but we have pretty much anything you might like."

Scott asked for a gin and tonic, and returned to business. What had started out as a ruse – the notion that his mission was just to get background for a story about cold war diplomacy shortly before the collapse of the Soviet Union

– was developing into an interesting story, and Scott had more or less convinced himself that with whatever he learned about Mary Evelyn he had the makings of an interesting if minor piece of history within his grasp. In any case, he turned to his main interest only after building some useful background information and then rounding stealthily to Mary Evelyn.

"Who were some of the people who worked with you? I've heard you liked to work with a small staff. How is your Russian, by the way?

"Not good enough for diplomacy, I'm afraid. We always took a translator with us, sometimes two."

"I'd like to speak with anyone in your group, but I heard they've either died or drifted off somewhere."

"I'm afraid so. John Cook died, Baker Fenster became an alcoholic and is in an institution somewhere, and our principal translator Mary Evelyn Klimov just dropped out of sight."

Harlan's scotch and soda had gone down in a hurry but was taking effect remarkably fast, and he soon warmed to the topic. He held out his glass, shaking the remaining ice, a signal for Cathy to attend to it. She did. "Cook was a big help, full of suggestions without getting in the way. Fenster, not so much. And Mary Evelyn wasn't just peripheral. She was a good-looking woman and quite charming. The Russians took quite a shine to her and that helped, especially in the evenings when we socialized with them. That created a positive climate for our discussions in Vienna."

"I wish I could talk to her. It would add some more background and color to the story. But I heard that she might have fallen victim to some killer in Rock Creek Park, where she often went running."

Harlan seemed to summon such reserves of caution as he had after taking a generous sip of his second cocktail. "I read about that stuff. I was out of town when she disappeared. I can't imagine why anyone would want to harm that sweet kid if it wasn't just some random crazy who did it." Scott detected a little watering of Harlan's eyes at that moment, but perhaps it was just the scotch at work.

After that Scott shifted back to the substance of Harlan's diplomacy and soon they proceeded to lunch in a sunlit room facing the pasture. "It's a light lunch, soup and sandwiches, but you can have seconds," Cathy offered. Harlan made short work of a sandwich and, as Cathy had foretold, seemed to be fading. The lids over his still-teary eyes were drooping and his head suddenly dropped to his chest, which brought him briefly back to alertness, but not for long. "I think I need to retire," he said thickly. Scott rose from the table and extended his and his thanks for Harlan's valuable assistance. "I should be going now," he said.

"Let me show you around the place first," Cathy said. "Give me a moment to change. I'm going for a ride this afternoon."

Scott waited in the living room. There were many pictures there of Harlan as a younger man. A quite handsome man, Scott saw, and very athletic looking. Many of the pictures, some of them taken with Cathy, showed them in riding gear, some on horseback, and there were a couple of them in skiing outfits.

Cathy showed up in jodhpurs and the same white blouse. "Let's go down to the barn. Have you ever seen a Thoroughbred close up? I'll show you some."

Scott wasn't particularly a fan of horses but he was too polite to say so, and he suspected that Cathy had something to tell him that wasn't about horses. "Little I know of horses, but this city boy doesn't often get the chance to meet a champion up close."

The stables, with their aroma of horse sweat and dung, could have accommodated twelve horses but there were only four. Two of them looked to be ordinary mounts but the other two were unusually tall and sleek. Cathy introduced Scott to one giant. "Cavalier, meet Mr. Sinclair."

Cavalier regarded Scott with gleaming and suspicious eyes. Cathy patted his head and stretched her face to his. They nuzzled like lovers, Scott thought. "You can rub his nose - feel how soft it is," Cathy said, as if granting him permission to kiss someone's hand. Scott tentatively reached out to touch the enormous beast and Cavalier drew back abruptly. He's taken my measure, Scott thought.

"Oh well, they can be a bit standoffish." He followed her into an adjacent room that doubled as a tack room and an office, well stocked with saddles, bridles and other gear, a desk on which there were several large ledger books, and two chairs. Cathy sat in one of them and motioned him to another.

"I'm going to tell you some things that Harlan wouldn't, but being in your business you would probably hear them anyway, and I want to be sure you hear our version. Or mine at least. There are some details that we might not agree on. And also," Cathy said, idly tapping a whip against her boot, "what's really important here is setting the record straight about Harlan and his work at the State Department. I think he got a raw deal, just because the work he was doing, exploring ways to ease tensions with the Russians, happened to fall out of favor, so that the very people who encouraged him to do it threw him under the bus and screwed up his career."

"That's the impression I'm getting already," Scott said. I certainly don't expect to write anything critical about him or his intentions."

"Good. But there's something else I expect you'll find out, if you're not already on to it, which I suspect you are, and I want you to have my own version and I just hope you will handle this whole business let's say delicately, the way you seemed to do with certain matters in your *New Yorker* article." In that expose, Scott had managed to refer to some private indiscretions in a manner sufficiently oblique as not to cause extreme embarrassment.

"That I promise." It was truthful enough, although he might share delicate matters plainly with Connie, because she was paying him to get to the truth.

"You showed interest in Mary Evelyn Klimov and I don't wonder since she up and disappeared in the middle of that whole mess, and she attracted a lot of attention, for obvious reasons, even before that. I know that she was playing a much greater role in those negotiations than Harlan let on, way beyond just translating. I think the

Russians liked her a lot, and so, frankly, did Harlan, and she reciprocated. I hope I'm not being too subtle here."

Scott shook his head gently and smiled, to indicate that he was getting her drift.

"That was when Harlan was married to Jane. And here comes my theory about Mary Evelyn's fate. Jane Hyde (that was her maiden name) came from an uptight conservative Midwestern family, and God knows why she and Harlan married each other. I married Harlan with my eyes open. She must have known he had lots of affairs. Maybe she thought she could reform him. I had no such illusions and it didn't matter to me particularly. But never mind that. The point is this: when she found out that Harlan was having an affair with Mary Evelyn, she just went nuts. I think she was borderline crazy to begin with, and that plus her righteous indignation about it just pushed her over the edge. She actually threatened to kill Harlan! She bought a gun but he managed to take it away from her. Then she made it clear that she meant to kill Mary Evelyn too. He thought he had dissuaded her but she dropped out of sight for a period when Mary Evelyn disappeared. I think Jane killed her or got someone to do it for her. She was one crazy bitch, I tell you. When she showed up again Harlan, who was having other troubles at work you may be writing about, decided he had had enough. There was a divorce and Jane went back to the comfort of her conservative family in Minnesota or wherever it was. I wouldn't be surprised if she wound up in an institution out there. So, there you have it."

"Wow," was all that Scott could offer. "Thanks for that background. Not that I plan to write about that. But other people are interested in what became of Mary Evelyn. I hope you're wrong about Jane trying to do away with her. We may never know."

They were about to leave the tack room when a man came through the door. "Say, Cathy, are you ready…" he began, but seeing Scott he abruptly altered conversational course. "Uh, Mrs. Van Horn…" He would have done less harm if he had said nothing.

"Ricky, this is Mr. Sinclair, our luncheon guest. I was just giving him a tour of the place. Scott, Ricky is our farm manager. And, as if to justify Scott's presence, said, "He's here to write a story about Mr. Van Horn's work at the State Department." There were awkward glances all around. Ricky was probably about 45, Scott thought, ruggedly handsome, wearing riding boots over his trousers and a polo shirt that emphasized his hard-muscled body.

"Uh huh," Ricky responded noncommittally. He was not sure how to behave in the current situation.

"I'm going to see him back to his car. I'll be back in a few minutes for our ride. Maybe you could saddle the horses for us now."

Ricky more or less recovered, or at least grasped the role he was supposed to play. "Okay, Mrs. Van Horn." He abruptly and awkwardly left the room, relieved that the encounter had come to an end.

As was Cathy. She explained. "Ricky is good with horses, and he helps out with other things around here." It would have been better, Scott thought, if she had said nothing. Left unsaid, Scott thought, was, "Ricky's not too bright, but just look at him."

"I'll walk you back to your car." While they walked, she offered some additional material, and gloss, for Scott's article. "Although I wouldn't have it said outright in front of him, Harlan had great prospects at the State Department. Then the administration decided that back channel efforts weren't yielding much and they shut down his operation. It just didn't make sense to them to be courting the Russians at the same time we were vilifying them so severely. So, he was quite unfairly tagged as soft on the Russians. That's why he left the State Department for the Council on Foreign Relations and to do some consulting work."

"Timing is everything, isn't it?" Scott said comfortingly. "It's a shame that your husband wasn't still in the Department when the wall came down and there was Gorbachev to deal with."

"Yeah. That eats him up still. I'm glad you understand."

Scott said goodbye and drove slowly out the long drive, through the estate gates and onto the road. He glanced over toward the stables. Cathy and Ricky were nearby on their horses, side by side with the animals facing each other, and the couple in conversation.

On the drive back to Washington Scott had plenty of time to ponder the complexity of human motivations and actions, and of some marriages.

Cathy had been clear-eyed when she married him. She knew well his history of philandering. That wasn't a welcome matter, but it bothered her little, even though she expected he would, sooner or later, repeat that behavior. In her calculations that would grant her a certain amount of marital license also, not that she had anything specific in mind, but she knew herself. The point was not to embarrass each other.

On the positive side, Harlan was handsome, fit, and vigorous, even if he was much older than she was. And wealthy. She had her own money and expected any groom to come to the altar with at least a similar endowment. Just as important – maybe more so – they were of the same class, not just moneyed but products of similar schools, members of the right clubs, intellectually inclined (they both thought) and socially active. They both liked horses. They both were readers of good literature, not the kind of junk some of her friends favored. And Harlan was connected to Washington political and governmental elites to which she previously had little access. Finally, Cathy liked him. He was witty and charming, and so long as his personal priorities and interests were not impaired, he was kind to her, although he was increasingly cranky and more withdrawn these days. A pre-nup had sealed the bargain – the ceremony confirmed it.

Now in her view Cathy was keeping up her end of the marital bargain, caring sympathetically for her infirm, tottering and dependent husband, even if their arrangement wasn't exactly something that she contemplated when they took their formal vows. In other words, Cathy was, after her own fashion, a good and loyal wife. Her loyalty included a firm commitment to preserve and enhance, if she could, her husband's reputation and public honor. She was quite willing to assist Scott's inquiries as long as she thought it would result in a broadly flattering portrait of her husband and his career. That career, which she admitted to herself had disappointingly fizzled within a year of their wedding, could use a bit of public buffing, and Scott was a means to that end.

She had made her bed and would lie in it. She had her horses (and Ricky), a place in the country she liked, the hired couple to meet their daily needs and to look after Harlan when she was visiting friends in New York and Philadelphia for shopping, seeing plays, or whatever. Things certainly hadn't turned out exactly as she had expected (do they ever?). Harlan's career had come to an end. He certainly was not the vigorous and cheerful fellow she married, and in fact he was aging at an alarming rate. Meanwhile she would do her duty. They were still compatible. Harlan had flashes of wit and wasn't entirely withdrawn from the world. He was aware that she was being kind to him, and in spite of his occasional ill-humor he was grateful for her understanding company, and said so. And she was grateful that he was.

Scott wondered how he would go about seeing if there was any substance to Cathy's theory about Harlan's first wife, Jane. He certainly wasn't going to go about it frontally. He decided to contact a Minnesota newspaperman he knew slightly, someone who had once manned a solitary Washington desk for his home paper and had gone back to become its editor. They had an introductory conversation and then Scott asked him if he knew anything about Jane Hyde or her family.

"I might not have known anything if it hadn't been that after she divorced her husband she came back here to live with her family. They had a lot of money from a seed business her grandfather started, and she inherited it. She was an odd duck and a difficult person. She decided she liked animals a lot more than people, so she started a kind of private zoo for exotic animals. The long and the short of it is that she got bitten by some kind of monkey and died of an infection, back, I guess, around 1980."

Another dead end, literally.

CHAPTER FOURTEEN

HELPING CONNIE, BLAIR, AND HIMSELF

Scott called Connie to give her an update on what he had been doing, and a sanitized version of what he had been told at Firewater Farm. He also wanted to sow a seed if he could.

After he told her about his trip to the farm, he said, "I'm mailing you a translation of the letter in the shoebox that was in Russian. It was from Mary Evelyn's mother, and it certainly suggests she was in big trouble when she disappeared, and not just from a furious woman."

"I'll read it with interest."

"How are you doing disposing of your excess furnishings?"

"Not great. I'm having trouble getting motivated. Is there anything you might like?"

"Thanks. My apartment is already at the edge of looking like a warehouse. But I do know some nice young people who might be interested in some of your unwanted things if they're not too pricey."

"Pretty much all I want is for someone to haul some of this stuff out of here. Why don't you bring them by sometime?"

Scott said he would get back to her. He called Blair at her office, left a message, and she called back.

"I hope you're not changing your mind about abandoning the Good Ends matter."

"No, I'm not. I'm pursuing a different matter right now, something that you might be able to help me with a bit." He briefed her on his Mary Evelyn project and asked if she could tell him what the Bureau thought – or knew.

"I'll let you know."

Then he turned to another matter. "Tell me, are you still interested in acquiring some quality furnishings on a bargain basis?"

"You bet. Are you getting rid of anything?"

"No, but I know someone who is."

He made the arrangements. The next weekend Blair and her husband Brian picked Scott up at his apartment and they drove out to Connie's place. Brian and Blair were wearing neatly pressed khaki slacks and white shirts. Off the job, Blair had allowed herself a little extra makeup and gold earrings.

Brian looked about six feet four inches and made of steel. He had a crew cut that emphasized a pair of outsized ears and a rubbery face that seemed primed for laughter. He was cheerful, well-mannered and enthusiastic. You could see that he would be a good teacher. He taught fifth grade math and coached several sports. Physically and otherwise the students would look up to him. His "aw, shucks" manner did not diminish the impression he gave that he respected himself and was a man to cope with all eventualities. Scott felt thankful that there were people like him who were willing to devote themselves to educating youngsters.

Connie gave them a warm greeting, anxious not to play the role of the grande dame. She was wearing jeans and a T-shirt with "NO PRISONERS!" emblazoned on the front, a gift, she said, from one of her daughters. She invited them to have something to drink in one of her "informal" rooms just to get acquainted. She asked a lot of questions about their work and their new house. She told them a little about her early days in Washington, working at Garfinkel's in Spring Valley, where she met and snared Jack when she waited on him in the department that sold china and glassware. Connie and the Blairs hit it off. She took them on a tour of the house, pointing out the things she meant to keep and those she didn't. Brian knew his way around a house, recognizing quality furnishings and what made them so, and suggesting, in a modest way, how she might deal with some household difficulties like balky appliances and sticky windows. Then she asked them to give her an idea of what they were looking for. With that done, they repeated their tour of the house. Connie suggested a number of things they might want to have, careful to say that she understood that these things might not fit their taste. They passed on the largest pieces offered – not enough room in their little house. After several items had been identified Brian said they ought to agree on prices because they might not be able to pay for them all.

"Here's my proposal," Connie said. "You come and pick these things up – you're responsible for moving them into a truck or whatever, and you can have them for nothing. But I'm not going to be responsible for that side of things. OK?"

"That's more than generous," Blair said. "We don't want to take advantage of you."

"Honey, no one takes advantage of me. Or at least not without paying a price for trying. You're friends of Scott, I'm a friend of Scott, and I like dealing with people I know. Besides, I like you, and I like what you both do. When can you bring a truck and a moving crew?"

And so, it was settled.

"God," Connie later said to Marge, "you and Blair Brown managed to get yourselves a couple of real men, the kind who don't need to affirm their manhood because it's obvious in the way they behave. I wonder if there are any more like them left. I mean closer to my age."

On the way back, with Brian driving, Scott gave Blair a copy of Potter's rough translation of Mary Evelyn's mother's letter. Blair read it, then read it again.

"I'd say from this letter and what you told me about the jealous wife and from Mary Evelyn's reckless way of living, like running alone in the park in the evenings, she may just have come to a bad end. The Bureau doesn't have any information about her death, but that doesn't mean it didn't happen.

"But," Scott said, "what do you think of some of the other things the letter hints at, involving the Russians?"

"Maybe she somehow became an inconvenience to the Russian delegation – or a single member of it – you know, something that grew out of all of that socializing they

115

were doing. She seems to have been the kind of woman who could drive men to do crazy things."

Scott called Connie later that day to thank her for helping Blair and Brian. Connie asked what he was going to do next. And what did he think?

"It's strange. I know a lot more than I did when I started out, but I just seem to be accumulating more questions as I go. I need to think about my next step. I'll let you know as soon as I have a plan."

"By the way," Connie said. "The letter jogged my memory a bit. When her mother said something about a roundabout way of writing to her, it was because the letter came in an envelope addressed to Mary Evelyn, inside another envelope addressed and mailed to me. I guess she was thinking someone would intercept a letter addressed to Mary Evelyn, don't you think?"

"It certainly sounds that way. And I don't think her mother was worried that Van Horn's wife or some crazy person in Rock Creek Park was the one who might do that."

Scott called Potter to relay this bit of information. Potter said he had something to share also. They made another date for lunch the next day, at Won's Szechuan restaurant.

"Thanks so much for the check, Scott. It certainly was more than I deserved, but I hope I can even the balance a bit today. Not that I have all of the answers, but I can fill in some useful background. You know, since the Russians decided to change their stripes, at least for a while, we've gotten access to a lot of their archives regarding espionage and statecraft, and there are a few bits that illuminate Mary Evelyn's situation."

"I'm all ears. Especially when my mouth is full of General Tso's chicken."

Potter interrupted his aggressive attack on his dish and on Scott's to share his findings. "In a nutshell, Mary Evelyn had several problems. In theory she might have become vulnerable to blackmail over her relationship with Van Horn, which the Russians were well aware of, but that probably didn't matter that much to her, although it would to him. But she had fallen into a trap with the Russians in two ways. First, did you know that she had a Russian father? Or had had, anyway. Apparently, the Russians got her to believe that he was still living and offered to help her get in touch with him. But whenever the Russians offer something, there is always a price. It starts off with asking for insignificant bits of information, but before you know if you've indiscreetly given them something you shouldn't have, and you're already compromised. I don't know what they promised but it was a lie. Her father died during the war. But how could she know that? They even gave her a letter purportedly written to her by him. So now she's already on the hook. They can warn her that they can let our side know that she's compromised. She might even have believed that. But worse, they had taken advantage of Van Horn's eagerness to score some kind of diplomatic coup by getting him to give them more information than he ought to have, believing he was advancing his negotiations by doing that. You would think an experienced diplomat would know better, but I expect he had the bit in his teeth and thought his diplomacy could vault him into State Department stardom. Stupid, you might think, and it was, but Van Horn wasn't the first clever person to be scuttled by his own ambition. And Mary Evelyn was caught in the same net, because Van Horn had used her for some of his purposes – she was the perhaps unwitting conduit for some of the information he was passing."

Potter paused to launch another assault on the table. Scott didn't say anything and waited for him to finish a few mouthfuls.

"But I suspect with her mother's counseling, at some point Mary Evelyn resisted further efforts by the Russians and started to disengage from Van Horn, for which she may have had several reasons. This made her a problem for the Russians. Not that losing her as a source of information was any great matter to them, but that she might spill the beans on Van Horn to the Feds, and that would have meant the loss of a potential asset well inside American diplomatic councils. So Mary Evelyn represented not much of an asset but potentially a great liability. And I'm sorry to say that probably led to her demise."

"You really think so?"

"You're welcome to believe that the Russians just got lucky and somebody murdered her in the park. Or that she defected to them, but that we would probably have learned long ago, and anyway she would not have fancied living in Moscow on a meager pension or something. I'm betting they did away with her in some quiet way, leaving no trace."

Potter paused. "And there's one last thing, which I think pretty much seals it. Around the time Mary Evelyn disappeared, a document shows that a Russian KGB assassin was briefly in town, and I don't think he was here on vacation."

Scott dreaded having to report this to Connie. So he decided not to, at least not right now. But he did tell Marge.

"I hate to say this, and I don't look forward to telling Connie, but Mary Evelyn is almost certainly dead, and dead for a long time. As if she didn't have enough threats from various other quarters, I just learned that she was likely assassinated by some Russian professional killer."

"How did you get that?"

"Well, that fellow Potter told me he learned there was such a guy in town around the time she disappeared. It adds up."

Marge paused a minute to pet Fay before sharing her opinion. "Has it occurred to you that she had too many enemies? I mean, so many people like that have come out of the woodwork, almost like there was a competition to claim responsibility. Maybe she's just in hiding somewhere."

"Maybe, but I don't think she could hide from the FBI. No, I'm afraid that the Russians got her. They had, as the police stories like to say, the means, the motive and the opportunity – I mean she was a sitting duck, like just about everyone here in Washington who doesn't have a security detail."

"Well, don't be in any hurry to tell Connie. It won't hurt her to wait until you're really sure."

"I think I'm about as sure as I'll ever get, but I'll hold off a while."

CHAPTER FIFTEEN

A LIVELY NIGHT AND A FRUITFUL MORNING

Scott had a lot on his plate. His quarterly newsletters had to be done soon. There were more people he needed to consult; more time needed just to think about the content of each letter. There were plenty of newsletters and services like his, except that his were meant to tell each client what the implications, short and long term, could be for its industry and its operations in particular, and that took a lot of thought. He was almost glad of the pressure he was under. It gave him something to think about besides Mary Evelyn's uncertain but likely grim fate.

It was Friday and he did not intend to forego a weekend with Marge, but he brought a full briefcase and his laptop computer.

Fay lay in her usual position, splayed out in the foyer. Sleep comes readily to a dog's untroubled conscience, and Fay, whose sense of guilt dissolved moments after being corrected for any misdemeanor anyway, was in deep slumber shortly after she had been admonished for presuming to take her ease on a living room sofa. But a dog's ears do not sleep, and the closing of the taxi door outside brought her quickly to her feet. Would it be?

Could it be Scott? The fact that he opened the front door with his own key sent her into a frenzy of anticipation. Yes! Fay nearly toppled Scott, resting her front paws on his extended hands by way of greeting, and Scott offered his left cheek to her outstretched tongue.

Marge came down the stairs offering Scott her own gentler greeting.

"I see you brought your work."

"Deadlines. I'll work while you're asleep."

"It's OK. I have my own tasks this weekend. After you and Fay have your fun, we get to have cocktails. I've got a steak ready to cook. Then guess what," she said, with a lascivious grin.

Scott embraced her and took her buttocks in his hands, pulling her toward him. "I'm looking forward to Fay, and the cocktails and dinner and the 'guess what'."

"In that order, tiger. Go play with Fay."

After cocktails, dinner, and a vigorous number three, Scott and Marge lay in bed.

"Are you really under the gun to get your newsletters out? You seemed a little distracted during dinner."

"No. I'm in pretty good shape there. I just have some finishing up to do. But I have had something on my mind. I've got to tell Connie that her friend Mary Evelyn is most likely dead, and I mean killed, back when she disappeared. She hired me to get information, and I can't justify holding it back forever."

"Yeah, that's going to be hard to take. Want me to do it?"

"No. Thanks, but it's my job. Besides, she'll want details."

"Are you really sure about this? I mean, how could you know?"

"I don't, but remember what I told you what that fellow Potter said. He has access to some Soviet archives. I think he's right, and I don't buy the story about Harlan's first wife doing it, and the murderer on the trail also seems a remote possibility too."

"But you don't know that for sure."

"No, but things add up."

"Sorry, darling. Maybe you don't need to tell Connie right away. Maybe some other news will turn up."

"Well I can't imagine what that could be."

Scott was astonished to see how unruly Michael McEvoy's courtroom was. He surveyed the room from his vantage point in the witness box. Behind the rows for attorneys and the accused, which were empty, the seats for visitors were just a blur, although there must have been people there because there was a great hubbub. On the bench Judge McEvoy dozed quietly. The jury box was full of mostly familiar faces, including Marge's. She looked at him dispassionately. Next to her in the front row was Harlan van Horn, head drooping onto Cathy Van Horn's shoulder. She was perusing a *New Yorker*. Robert Potter was holding a notebook while listening to whispers of the man next to him, a sturdy looking fellow wearing a cap with a red star above the brim. Roger Harrington sat quietly, shaking his head gently as though he had just discovered a potentially libelous statement in some draft article by Scott. At the end of the row was a stern looking woman who wore a safari jacket and fidgeted with her purse. On the row behind, Blair and Brian Brown were seated together earnestly discussing something, perhaps furnishings, but they never took their eyes off Scott. Next to them was an unknown figure who was scouring the courtroom and busily taking notes of something or other, and at his side was another man wearing a striped pants and shirt outfit. At the end of that row was Dottie McEvoy beaming toward her husband. A jury, fittingly, of twelve.

In front of Scott was Connie, who stood with arms folded. "I want some answers!" she demanded.

Scott found himself replying, "I don't have any. Just a bunch of dead ends."

Connie turned her back on him in disgust. Then she pointed to the doors at the rear of the courtroom, one of which opened to allow Mercury to ride his bicycle down the center aisle. He had a hard time keeping his balance because he was carrying a large and heavy object in the satchel slung over his back, but he managed to reach a place next to Scott's witness box, against which he parked his bicycle. Then he unburdened himself of the satchel and emptied its contents onto the floor: a beautiful young woman wearing shorts, a T-shirt, and running shoes. As she struggled to her feet Scott saw Harlan Van Horn come very much to life, smiling and tearing up. Cathy patted his knee and handed him a cocktail glass. The fidgety woman seemed very agitated and gave the young woman a cross look. Robert Potter set aside his notebook and gave the woman an admiring once-over. Roger was stone-faced, his still unflappable self. Blair and Brian gave up talking about furnishings to exchange knowing looks. The man in the striped outfit looked as if he understood everything and the man with the cap looked disappointed.

As the young woman arose Scott and everyone else noticed that she was missing her left hand. Connie, again facing Scott, gave him a look that said, "Well?" Then she turned and pointed at the door at the rear of the room through which Fay trotted and made her way down the aisle until she reached the woman, whereupon Fay dropped a hand from her mouth. The young woman daintily picked up the hand and reattached it to her wrist and then patted Fay's head and neck. Fay assumed her usual sphinxlike position on the floor. The courtroom (including roughly half of the jury) and the unseen visitors erupted in applause.

Suddenly Judge McEvoy asserted control, banging his gavel for order and then using it (the gavel had a handle the length of a golf club) to tap Scott on the shoulder.

"Wake up, Scott! You've been babbling your head off about Mary Evelyn and saying a bunch of other names and thrashing around. Are you OK?"

Scott could only reply that he must have been thinking about Mary Evelyn because he felt so frustrated by his failure to determine what exactly had happened to her, although he feared the worst. The dream that had seemed so vivid had dissolved upon his awakening.

Marge patted his head, as she would Fay's." I expect you'll get to the bottom of it eventually."

Scott doubted it. He went back to sleep and the dream did not return.

When he woke up the next morning Scott found himself alone in bed. He went downstairs in his bathrobe and found Marge, wearing jeans and a T-shirt, in her study at her computer.

Scott patted Fay good morning and kissed Marge. "School business you need to work on?"

"Something much more important. Get your coffee and have a seat."

When he returned with his coffee Marge asked, "Ready for some good news?"

"The good news is that I'm here with you and Fay."

"This is better. I've been busy doing research. Sit down. How many 'Mary Evelyns' do you suppose are on college faculties around the country? Teaching Russian language and literature?"

Scott's jaw dropped. "One would be enough."

"Well, there's a Dr. Mary Eleanor Dowd teaching those subjects at a college out in California."

"Close, but no cigar. She's Mary Evelyn." But as soon as he said this, he remembered Mary Evelyn's sister. "My God! You're a genius!"

"Women's intuition. It just struck me that Mary Evelyn might have taken her mother's advice to make haste and got herself out of town before anything bad could happen to her. And what would she do with herself to make a living? She had an M.A. in Russian language and literature. Translating work would be what she had been doing but would probably make her easier to track and find. So I started looking online for faculty members teaching Russian. It only took an hour or so while you were snoozing."

"This is great even though it makes me feel really stupid for not doing what you did. Of course, we can't be certain. It could be a coincidence."

"There's only one way to find out. But we need to consult Connie first, don't you think?"

They did. Connie was elated and wanted to pay Scott more than he deserved and he refused anyway to accept anything. Besides, it was Marge who cracked the case.

CHAPTER SIXTEEN

SCOTT GETS HIS STORY

Connie invited them for lunch on a Sunday, in the house she expected soon to vacate. "Not formal," she emphasized, so they arrived in slacks and sweaters – it was the first cool day of the approaching fall season. Connie welcomed them, saying "Clara has the day off, so I brought in a new cook," as she led them into the kitchen. The cook, wearing an apron over her blouse and plaid skirt, put aside a bowl she was stirring something in, wiped her hands on a dishcloth and stepped forward to greet them. "Hi, I'm Mary. I've heard a lot about you both."

It took only a few seconds for Scott to recognize her from the photos. A beautiful woman may show her age, but she will usually remain beautiful. She was tall, ash blond and pretty, and still willowy. She hadn't lost her looks, and Scott could see through the surprisingly slight effects of age the woman in the picture in the newspaper and the photograph.

"It's you, isn't it?"

She ignored the idiocy of his question. "Yes and no. I am, or I was, Mary Evelyn Klimov. Now I'm Mary Eleanor, and my married name is Dowd." For good reasons I've just gone by 'Mary' for a long time.

"I'll be damned!" Marge exclaimed.

"I doubt it. Not from what Connie tells me about you. I've really been eager to meet you."

"I convinced her to come here for a visit," Connie explained. "Of course, she's sort of incognito. We're staying away from places like the Sulgrave Club where people might recognize her."

Mary cheerfully turned to her tasks. "You can have your choice of grilled cheese sandwiches or a grapefruit and avocado salad. Or both. "

"Have a seat while we work our kitchen magic here," Connie said. "I told you this would be informal." She directed them to the bar stools at the kitchen island. "When we sit down to eat Mary can tell you her story, which I'm sure you're eager to hear. I convinced her to come here so that we could revisit old times and I could show her around a bit. I think it's safe for her to be here in DC if we keep a low profile. You'll notice that she's still a beauty, and people don't forget a face like that."

"A pair of dark glasses and my graying hair are all the camouflage I need, I think. We're almost done here. And I want to know more about you two. So, you'll have to sing for your supper as well."

Mary moved around the kitchen with an expert's ease, and a meal was soon served in a kitchen nook. She uncorked a bottle of white wine and poured for everyone. She raised her glass. "Here's to you two detectives, and especially to discretion, which Connie assures me I can count on. And with that assurance, I'll tell you what you may not know already and whatever else you want to know. Between bites, of course."

"How did you manage to elude everyone, including the Feds, and reinvent yourself? And if it isn't too intrusive, why did you have to? I have some notions about that but I could be wrong."

Mary responded to Scott's question. "I won't hold anything back, but if you don't mind, it might be better if I started further back, because family history helps explain how I got into such a fix."

"Go ahead."

When Mary finished her sandwich, she did.

CHAPTER SEVENTEEN

ORIGIN STORY

"I'm going to give you the unabridged version, maybe more than you want, but I sort of want to tell my story and I've never been able to tell it all to anyone before, except most of it to my husband. He's an understanding man and we have a great marriage. He's the dean of students at the college where I teach. I have not told my two sons the whole story – I mean about some of my behavior as a young woman. You understand."

"Of course."

"My story starts about a century ago when my grandparents emigrated from Russia to the U.S. They came from an area near Finland – I guess it might have been part of Finland at some point, the way borders shifted back and forth then. Anyway, they were members of a large family that all left Russia pretty much at the same time to seek a better economic life and also because they were some kind of socialists who thought America held better prospects for socialism than Russia did. That was around the turn of the century.

"They – the men anyway – were skilled workers, machinists most of them, and they thrived in Wisconsin where they eventually landed. But then came the Russian revolution and like many well-meaning people they swallowed the communist line and a few of them including my grandparents with my mother in tow went back to Russia to help 'build socialism' using their skills. Of course, nothing went as promised or hoped for, but there was no going back. So there they were. My grandparents made a point of raising my mother to be bilingual. Where they settled the schools were pretty decent, it being a community with a lot of engineers and scientists, and my mom absorbed a lot of culture, did well in school, and when the time came she was sent to a university where there was a good foreign language and literature department although overlaid with a lot of communist ideology. After she finished school, she became a translator attached to some state commercial apparatus that dealt with foreigners. Mom was a shrewd person and she kept a lid on her hatred of communism and all of its works, and at the same time she idealized the U.S., her birth country. She still had a U.S. passport.

"She was about 30 years old and had married a man who disappeared during the 'Great Patriotic War' as the Russians called World War II. It never was clear to her what became of him, whether he died in some battle (he was some kind of junior officer) or otherwise. Things were so tumultuous then that there was just no telling what happened. And then she was pregnant, with me and my sister. She resolved to get out of Russia and go back to the United States. Much more easily said than done!"

Mary Evelyn paused and sipped her wine. "Maybe this is more than you wanted to know, but it's background for what happened later to me. Anyway, with war raging to east and west she decided to try going south, I think without a clear itinerary, but she had a native wit, fierce determination, and a U. S. passport, so she struck out, using any means of transportation that presented itself, hitchhiking rides on trucks, taking trains and even riding in a cart pulled by some draft animals. The people she met along the way must have been a lot more chivalrous than the average Russian, but even they can be sympathetic and helpful to a woman who is obviously pregnant. I believe she got help from some friends at the U. S. Embassy in Moscow and then U. S. consulates along the way, maybe a little financial assistance since she was a U.S. citizen in distress. Otherwise I can't understand how she made it.

"The journey was in two stages – before my sister and I were born, and after. Mom was a remarkable woman who had quantities of courage and resourcefulness, plus a lot of luck. She started with a plan to go to Turkey and then somehow to drift across the Mediterranean and out to the Atlantic. That plan fell apart almost at once when she couldn't get the necessary transportation, and she would be crossing war zones too. Her guiding notion seemed to be just to keep moving at all costs, which considering her pregnancy was probably wise. In Moscow she managed to talk her way onto a military flight to Orenburg, down there at the bottom of the Urals. At least that took her a long way from Moscow in a more-or-less southerly direction. I'm not sure she had a very detailed notion of the geography she was transiting. She told me that she took a train from there, in a freight car I think, to Tashkent, and somehow got a lift on an airplane to Kabul. It got a little fuzzy from there but by road or rail she made it to Islamabad, and then onto a train headed to Delhi, then on by rail to Goa, which was a Portuguese colony down on the Malabar coast of India.

"But I'm getting ahead of myself, because by the time she got to Islamabad she had been travelling for several months and was running out of steam because she was due to give birth in a couple of weeks. It was there, as the novelists say, that fate took a hand. On the train to Delhi with her was a Catholic nun who was headed for Goa. She was at hand when my mother gave birth to me and my sister, and having some rudimentary nursing skills she managed to see that we were delivered safely. We came

140

through it amazingly well. Mom at this point needed a lot of help so she readily agreed to go on with this nun to Goa, where she figured she might find a boat that would take the three of us to the U.S."

Mary paused and took a sip of wine. "Don't worry, we're getting close to the end of this ancient history."

"Take your time. This is fascinating."

"Now this nun had, not exactly as a price or condition for help, but as a reasonable request that would have been hard to refuse even if my mother had had any misgivings, that my sister and I would be baptized in a Catholic church in Goa. And so, we were. I think Mom was agnostic, but since the Communists were so hostile to the notion of God and were so wrong and deceitful about everything else, she thought there might be something in Christianity. Anyway, this nun marched my mother with us to a priest in a church where he was doing baptisms.

"Mom said I was the first up, maybe because I was the first out. The priest said 'Name this child' and my mom said 'Evelyn'. (She had known an Evelyn somewhere and liked the name.) The priest said, 'There is no Saint Evelyn. She needs a saint's name.' Mom looked up, and there was a statue of the Virgin Mary. 'OK, Mary Evelyn' and for good measure she added a 'Mary' to my sister Eleanor's

141

name – she had heard about Eleanor Roosevelt and admired her for her pluckiness and strength. So that's how we came to be the two 'Marys'."

Scott interjected, "I wonder what your birth certificate would have said as to place of birth, something like 'en route between Islamabad and Goa'."

"It turns out that not having a birth certificate, but just naturalization papers after getting back to this country, was a sort of benefit, but I'm getting to that phase in a minute.

"There may have been a consulate or something in Goa to help her but at least somehow Mom managed to book passage to Cape Town, I think working as a cook, a step in the right westerly direction and, as I said, her idea was to keep moving toward her goal by whatever means she could, so after a couple of weeks convalescing in a convent in Goa we were on our way again. In Cape Town she connected with a U.S. consulate that helped her for a while and from there she got a boat – maybe a series of boats – that took her to Buenos Aires and from there up to the U. S. I don't really know many details but we landed eventually in D. C. where Mom figured she might find work as a translator, which she did. And there she raised me and Eleanor to be bilingual, thinking that we could always make a living with our language skills, and right she was."

Mary Evelyn paused to take a few bites of her salad. "Maybe that was too much background."

Scott thought she seemed very relaxed and cheerful in her manner for someone telling a life story that she had taken great care to hide for many years.

Mary gave Scott a description of the work she had done with Van Horn, not adding very much to what he already knew about their discussions with the Russians. "But I suppose you want to know what happened to me specifically. It's a long story. I'll tell you just about everything but I don't want you take notes or anything. OK?"

"I came without a notebook. As promised, my lips are sealed. But I brought you something that may help you to jog your memory. He presented her with the entire contents of the shoebox in a large manila envelope he had intended to return to Connie. Mary Evelyn read quickly the letters from her sister and mother, and the notes from "H". "I have a rough translation of your mother's letter, done by a discreet person."

"Thanks. I can't believe I left these things behind, but my mother's letter certainly shows how anxious I was to get out of town. These certainly bring back memories, and when I re-read them when I'm alone I expect to have a good cry over them. I felt terrible that I had to leave Connie and other people with no goodbyes and no explanation. I also left her with my share of the rent to be paid. I guess that debt has gathered a lot of interest over the years, but I'll make good on it, whether the money matters to her or not."

Mary Evelyn explained how she found herself working as a translator and the diplomatic work she participated in with Van Horn. She again asked and received confirmation from Scott that from here on in he would keep to himself the more intimate matters and also any that might incriminate her or damage her reputation to the point of jeopardizing her job at the college and embarrassing her and her family. Especially the intimate matters.

"As you can tell from my mother's letter, I was in deep trouble."

"Because of your involvement with Harlan? I've heard his wife was fiercely jealous and angry – even to the point of trying to do you harm."

Mary laughed "She was sort of nutty to begin with, but I never expected she would try to do me any physical harm until Harlan told me she had bought a gun he took away from her. He would have been her first victim anyway. But she was the least of my worries. Now here is where I need to be extremely careful about what I say. Let's just say that I had gotten on very well with the Russian diplomats we were negotiating with. There was a lot of socializing in Vienna, and although there was nothing about that in my contract with the State Department as a translator it was clear that it had become part of my job. And I liked doing it. I'm an outgoing person."

Yes, Scott thought, and you were a very fetching one too. Even now, past the bloom of youth, she was a very good-looking woman, and an engaging personality.

"Two things, quite apart from my affair with Harlan I had done (to be blunt about it) that got me in hot water. First, at Harlan's direction, and thinking foolishly that it was just part of the complex process of diplomacy, I was passing a lot of information to the Russians, mostly by voice. I was very slow to realize how tricky a business that was. Worse, the Russians we were talking to turned out to know a lot about me and my family – more than I did. And more than was true, it turned out. At a certain point I was taken aside and told that my father was still living. The fed me a story about how he had gotten separated from his military unit, was captured by the Germans, and finally released long after my mother had left the country.

145

Looking back now I'm amazed that I swallowed that story. They suggested that I could get in contact with him, eventually with a rendezvous somewhere, and as further bait they gave me a letter he purportedly wrote to me. Then at each interval where they fed me more bait some innocent slice of information was solicited from me, and then by the time I realized what a fool I was (under my mother's instruction) I was already technically compromised. It's hard to explain how I could have been so naïve, but the prospect of connecting with one's hitherto unknown father has a powerful pull. I actually thought that my mother would be delighted with me, but she immediately saw what nonsense it was and how I was being used and probably setting myself up for a prison sentence in the U. S. She gave me hell.

"Then there was another strand. Harlan, I now think, was even more compromised than I was. Now Harlan was a very intelligent, experienced and savvy person, but I think his judgment was clouded by ambition. He thought, and he confided it to me, that we were on the brink of some major diplomatic breakthrough and that he would be covered in glory when it happened. So, he too found that he had been too forthcoming with information to the point that an outside observer would conclude that his discussions with the Soviets went beyond indiscreet and were tinged with treason.

"By the way, what's become of Haran? I understand he left the State Department, but after that I lost track. I also heard he divorced. I'm afraid I had a role in that. Anyway, what's become of him?"

"I saw him a few months ago. He's not in great shape physically but he seems to well looked after by his second wife."

"I'm happy for that at least. Anyway, that's a long-closed chapter.

"Now as I said I was his innocent but really stupid instrument in this also. I told him about my concerns, and he counseled me to say nothing, but I think he knew I was likely to save my own skin and throw myself at the mercy of the authorities, and then he would be in much deeper trouble. Dumb as I had been, it finally started to dawn on me that I could be very inconvenient to Harlan and therefore to the Russians. When I revealed all of this to my mother, she was furious with me and berated me terribly, saying she couldn't believe she could have raised such a stupid daughter. But she was also terrified for me. And that's when we concocted my disappearance and my escape to a new life.

CHAPTER EIGHTEEN

"WHERE NO MAN PURSUETH"

Mary smiled appreciatively and finished off her meal, the last of them to do so as she had been doing most of talking while the others ate. Connie refilled her glass. "Why don't you all retire to the living room while I tidy up here," Connie suggested. "I won't be long, and I've heard the whole story already."

Marge, Scott and Mary did as suggested, Mary bringing her glass with the last of the wine with her. "I've earned this, I think. I can make this story long or short, and you can interrupt me whenever you feel like it, and you can tell me when you've had enough. OK?"

Marge and Scott nodded. They were both eager to get the entire story.

"It was my mother's ingenious scheme. First, my sister had died of cancer a few weeks earlier. We looked quite a bit alike, but more important, we were both 'Mary E's' so that I was able to slip rather easily into her identity except for the part about her being a nun – I just dropped that out of my resume – which worked nicely because the church had put her through graduate school so that she could teach at a Catholic university and be a resource for the church in any mission to a Russian-speaking place, plus she nearly mastered some other Eastern European languages like Czech and Hungarian.

"I took my mother's advice and just walked out of our apartment one morning with nothing but a shopping bag with a handful of toiletries and a change of underwear. I had to make it look as though my disappearance was unplanned and that I was kidnapped or killed or something. I always kept a few clothes at Mom's place so I had enough to get me by for a while. I hopped on a Greyhound bus and waved goodbye to my old life forever. I felt rotten – I still do – leaving Connie and other people flat and worrying about me but Mom insisted on it, and she was wise to do so. My mother's resourcefulness rescued me. At that time she was working as a librarian at the University of Wisconsin where some people she knew were looking for a companion for their elderly mother. In terms of availability I was just the ticket. The woman lived by herself in a large house. All I had to do was prepare meals and keep her company for the part of the day when she was up and about, which was only about five hours a day. In those periods I mostly read to her, which I enjoyed doing. One morning, after I had been holed up there for several months, I went to wake her up and she wouldn't. She died. By that time, I had been lying low long enough for my trail to grow cold, and I was ready to move on. But where?

"While I was staying with the old lady, I was never idle – it's not my nature – and I was planning my next move. I researched jobs in my field and stumbled across a position at the University of Alaska where they needed someone to translate Russian documents to English for some historians. You know the Russians had Alaska until we bought it from them, so that history was of special interest in those parts. Well, if you want to get yourself lost to the world in a place where people don't ask too many questions about your past, Alaska's just the thing. Then, exercising my skills and using my sister's academic resume which was quite similar to my own, I was able to gravitate into academia, and get a PhD. And that's where I met my husband, Frank. We wound up teaching together a couple of decades ago in California and there we are, we and our two sons. So, there you have it."

"If I may say so, that's a hell of a story. I wish I could write about the whole thing, but of course I can't, and won't.

CHAPTER NINETEEN

A TURNING POINT

It was Scott's practice to call Marge every evening that they were not together, if she did not call him first, to recount notable or diverting events of their days, to inquire into each other's wellbeing, and to exchange thoughts about books, people, or the daily news, all to compensate for physical absence. These conversations could occupy as much as an hour, or only a few minutes if either of them had tasks to perform which could not be fit into their normal routines. This night Marge's phone rang repeatedly, almost to the point of the answering machine taking charge, when Marge's voice, normally bright and enthusiastic, gave a muffled greeting. "Hi, Scott."

"What's wrong?"

It was as if a stopper had been pulled from a vessel of grief. "Fay died. Some men working in the back garden left the gate open and she got loose. She got hit by a truck. Oh, Scott, I'm so miserable." And then she sobbed.

"I'm coming right over."

"You don't have to."

"I'm coming anyway."

Scott took a taxi straight out, meanwhile figuring out how he should adjust the next day's schedule so that he would not have to rush off in the morning. After the first half-hour of consoling conversation he ordered Chinese take-out and fixed them both a martini. They had several, ate the Chinese delivery meal, and went to bed. She fell asleep in his arms. There was no thought of sex. Marge mourned herself to sleep while Scott remained awake for some time. Something had happened. He didn't know whether it came about because of Marge's display of vulnerability or his realization, or the intensity of his realization, that Marge's happiness or lack of it meant so much to him. He wanted the day to think about it. He did go back to his apartment the next morning after Marge had dragged herself into her school. He made a few calls on his sources and headed back out to her place in the afternoon.

That evening, with a roast in the oven and their cocktails in hand, on the sofa together, Scott said, "I think you should get another dog. I know it's early but you need it for protection, and for company."

"I don't want another dog now. I want Fay, and I can't have her back."

"In that case, I'll have to do. I want to marry you. Or I want you to marry me. I'm never sure of the proper formulation. Will you?"

Marge hesitated. "You're just overcome by the emotion of the moment. Trying to be nice to me."

"I mean it, darling. You know I adore you, and I love how happy you make me. I love my work but I've gotten so that I dread it when the weekend is over and I have to go back to town. And I want to make you happy too, if I can. Do you remember your – our- dinner party last June with Mike and Dottie and Connie and Roger, when we went around the table trying to think of things that we did that showed off our best selves? Everyone had done something positive for other people, and showed they were caring people. And what they did brought them great happiness. Except for me. All I could come up with was something I hadn't done. But now I can do something that would bring me great happiness and I hope make you happy too. I don't mean I want to interfere in your life – we're both very independent people. I just want to make you happy and safe, or as safe as we can be in this life, and to do that permanently. And I would make myself even happier. So, will you marry me?"

"I'll have to think about it." Marge stared at her folded hands.

"I understand." He did, but his disappointment was clear.

"OK. I've thought about it. Yes!" Marge laughed with tears in her eyes, and launched herself into his lap.

Marge wiped her eyes, and produced another round of tears. When that was done, she resumed the subject. "We'd have to make some adjustments, you and I. I mean, do we live here or at your place or somewhere in between?"

"We can stay here, close to your school, and you can drop me off at the Metro station when I have to go downtown."

"But what about your condominium, and your precious furnishings?

"I've got too much furniture anyway. And this house is big enough for a family of six. There are five bedrooms for God's sake! I'd like to take the large spare bedroom overlooking the garden and set that up as my office and sitting room with a few cherished items from my place."

"Nevertheless, I have my conditions."

"Such as?"

"Separate checkbooks and credit cards. I don't want you scrutinizing my every expenditure and telling me I paid too much, or shouldn't have spent the money at all. Thank God I have my own money, and you have yours."

When she told Connie the news, she shared a little concern with her. "I just wish it hadn't been, you know, precipitated by losing Fay, as though he proposed just because he felt sorry for me."

"Scott isn't the kind of person to act on impulse. He would have proposed eventually anyway. So, don't look a gift horse in the mouth. Don't you realize that he adores you? Will you ever get a chance like this for happiness the rest of your life? There must have been dozens of women he dated he might have proposed to, but I'll bet he never did, or they would have leapt at the chance. Look, you have everything in common, especially your values, which count more than anything else."

Marge didn't really need to be prompted to marry Scott. But who doesn't appreciate some reassurance that what they want to do is the right, and the obvious thing to do? Now she had it.

CHAPTER TWENTY

NOT SO SMART AFTER ALL

Blair and Brian Brown invited Scott, Marge and Connie to lunch one Saturday afternoon. They wanted to show off their newly furnished and somewhat redecorated house, and to show their appreciation for their benefactors. They also wanted to celebrate Scott and Marge's engagement.

The five of them sat around a table in their tiny patio. Brian, who was the person in the household with the superior cooking skills, had made them crab crepes with oyster sauce, with a sauvignon blanc, much to everyone's delight and surprise. After lunch, as they were leaving, Blair asked Scott if he could linger a bit while Marge and Connie were going off shopping. They went back to the patio and Brian excused himself to clean up the kitchen.

"How was Mary Evelyn, or Eleanor as she is now?"

Scott's jaw dropped. "You knew?"

"Do you think you could find her but we couldn't? Come on! We knew pretty much every step of the way where she was. Now this is for your information only: She couldn't be prosecuted without also prosecuting Van Horn, who didn't have quite the excuse of naivete that she could claim. And the government decided not to go after Van Horn for multiple reasons. First of all, these cases are tricky to prosecute. Too much sensitive information can get spilled if you want to get a conviction – and you might or might not get it anyway. And the whole case would make the government look stupid. Finally, Van Horn had his uses, including passing a little disinformation to the Russians from time to time, even after he left the department."

"You could have just told me all of this and saved a lot of trouble," Scott pouted.

"And hand you a dead fox? And how did we know then that we could trust you not to reveal things we weren't anxious to get out. We're not in the business of unnecessarily meddling in people's lives, no matter what people think. Anyway, it was convenient for the government to have her disappear, even though we didn't have a hand in that, except for just letting her go."

"And how did you know we met her?"

"She told us. We've been in contact for years now. When the Van Horn business blew over, we got in contact with her. We found her up in Alaska. We told her to continue to lie low, for everyone's sake, and she'd be left alone. She knows how to be close-mouthed by now. She asked if it would be OK to come back to DC, and we said she could make a short visit as long as she kept a low profile."

"I feel like such a dope."

"No, you were just left out of the loop. I hope you won't hate me for this. You have been wonderful to me and Brian, you and Connie. I don't feel good about what I've had to do. If we hadn't trusted both of you, you know, we might have found a way to derail your efforts, maybe by telling you that Mary Evelyn was dead and that we knew but couldn't tell you how."

"And what about Bob Potter? He knows?"

"He didn't. When necessary the Bureau and the Agency share information, but not always. There was no need for him to know. Since we figured you might fill him in now, we've recently had a little chat with him. We're not worried about him. He's a trooper."

Scott couldn't help feeling used.

"And you might as well know, there was another person who knew: Stanley Greene. He was getting a little too close to the truth when he investigated Mary Evelyn's disappearance, so we had a chat with him. He agreed to keep quiet about what he was learning about her involvement with the Russians and even to push the story about how she probably got killed in Rock Creek Park. Actually, we made a bargain with him. We offered him a few small dead foxes."

"Unbelievable," Scott said glumly. I've been duped by everyone."

"I didn't lie to you. I just said we didn't have any information about her death. OK, it wasn't the whole truth. But I really had no choice. I can't go around spilling secrets just because I like someone or because I'm indebted to them. Don't feel bad. You – and Marge – got to the truth on your own. And you can still write a sanitized article, or even a book, about back-channel diplomacy, just without certain details."

CHAPTER TWENTY-ONE

DENOUEMENT

Scott eventually wrote his book-length article about American back-channel diplomacy, going back to the early years of the Republic. The *New Yorker* turned it down but he found a publisher and it sold well. Scott was a good story-teller. And although he continued to thrive in his work, he was a little less cocky than he was at the beginning of the year 2000.

Scott and Marge were married between Christmas and New Year's Day, with only a few close friends and Scott's son Andrew in attendance. Scott did move to Marge's house and they managed their separate work lives and financial affairs with no difficulty. They got a dog - it was the one thing Scott demanded, because he couldn't go running with Marge all of the time. The dog was a Doberman, and like Fay, friendly and devoted to both of them, but not a dog to be crossed by strangers.

Connie moved to a house in the fashionable Kalorama section of Washington, where she had a series of boyfriends, but that never went anywhere because none of them could handle a woman of Connie's will and independence. Finally, she got a dog too, a tiny Havanese, just for companionship. Connie never felt she needed protection.

Blair and Brian Brown sold their small home and moved to the suburbs after they had their first baby and needed more space.

Harlan Van Horn died early in 2001. Cathy continued to live on the farm, with regular visits to New York for "R and R". Ricky grew a little too presumptuous after Harlan's death and Cathy evicted him from the farm.

Mary Evelyn/Eleanor returned to her family. She decided that her sons deserved to get the full story of her life. They were unfazed; in fact, proud.

"Good Ends" came to a bad end for many of the people involved. A New York Times reporter who was also on the case accepted a dead fox promise and was duly rewarded. He broke the story and became a Pulitzer runner-up.

Robert Potter, in partnership with Won, started a new business selling novelty fortune cookies to Chinese restaurant owners willing to test their patrons' sense of humor. Here are some of the "fortunes" those customers found in their cookies.

Someone in this room is stalking you!

There is no statute of limitations on that thing
you did.
You are being audited by the IRS. Time to lawyer
up.
You will have many lovers. Too bad about the
STD.
Have you considered cosmetic surgery?
Your doctor wants to see you. Something about
test results best discussed in person.
You turned off all of the kitchen appliances you
needed to before you left home today - or did
you?

They did not make much money out of this enterprise,
but Robert felt they had struck a blow against triteness
and for comedic liberty.

Author's Note

Some years ago I found myself at a dinner seated at a table among strangers. A woman of about sixty seated next to me introduced herself as Mary Evelyn Something-or-other. I complimented her on her name and mentioned that the name "Mary Evelyn" appears in my family tree. "Actually," she said, "it was only supposed to be Evelyn, but the Mary part got tacked on when I was christened." I asked her about that. "Are you ready for kind of a long story?" I was, and she told it to me.

It was the core of my novel's story about Mary Evelyn, how her grandparents emigrated to America from Russia and migrated back to Russia after the 1917 revolution with Mary Evelyn's young mother; how that mother, with a Russian husband lost in World War II, and pregnant with Mary Evelyn, made her way out of Russia and eventually back to America, giving birth to Mary Evelyn *en route* in India. I have embellished the tale of course, not least by giving my Mary Evelyn a twin, but the essential adventure is based on that remarkable history.

Authors often ritually assert that no character in their stories is based on anyone living or dead, and they may mean it, but I don't see how any character can be created out of nothing, because even imagination has to be based on experience. In this case I make no such assertion. I stole the back story from the original Mary Evelyn. I hope she doesn't mind.

About the Author

Felton McLellan ("Mac") Johnston's career has involved military intelligence, international banking, political risk insurance, and international investment risk consulting. A native Washingtonian, he served in official capacities in the Federal Government for over two decades. He continues to observe, from his perch in nearby Bethesda, Maryland, the inner workings of official Washington and its numerous camp-followers, viewing with admiration the commonly overlooked acts of dedication, professionalism, and occasional courage of great numbers of individuals in the so-called deep state.

Made in the USA
Coppell, TX
24 March 2020